CRUSH 3

TEXT **KINGPUB** to **22828** to join the **King Publishing Group** mailing list!

Free book giveaways, event dates and much more!

CRUSH 3

IVY SYMONE

Chapter 1

Jazmin let out a frustrated breath of air as she tried to hold back her tears. The emergency room staff was trying to be discreet and comforting without being alarming. Jazmin knew what was going on. She didn't even bother questioning the radiology technician while he performed the ultrasound. His assistant awkwardly tried distracting her from looking at the monitor by asking dumb questions. Jazmin knew what they were doing.

Now, she waited in her exam room along with Tanya for the doctor to come in and officially diagnose her with a miscarriage.

"It's gonna be okay, Jazz," Tanya consoled.

"So, what happens now?" Jazmin sniffled. "Do I just bleed it out?"

Tanya's eyes widened. "The hell if I know! Why you asking me as if I done had a miscarriage before?"

"Well, I thought...well, you know..." Jazmin stammered with awkwardness.

"No, I don't know," Tanya retorted, feigning insult.

Jazmin snickered, "My bad."

"I know yo' bad."

Jazmin was about to respond but her phone rang. She frantically retrieved it, almost dropping it in the process. It was an unfamiliar number but she was hoping it was who she was waiting to hear from. She answered it eagerly.

"Hello?"

"Are you okay?" asked Desiree.

Jazmin sighed with disappointment. She was expecting to hear from Jah but he had yet to call her. She had to know if he was okay.

She answered, "No, I'm not. I'm miscarrying."

Desiree gasped. "I'm so sorry, Jazz."

"Yeah," Jazmin said in a depressed tone.

"Well, what about Jah? What's happening with him? Georgia told me everything when I picked Genni up."

"I don't know. You call Daddy?"

"I tried but he wasn't answering," Desiree said.

"Okay, let me make a few calls. And as soon as I'm done here I'll be on my way to get Genni," Jazmin told her.

As soon as the call ended, the glass sliding door to the exam room slid open. Expecting to see the doctor or a nurse, instead, Jazmin was surprised to see Lamar stepping around the corner of the privacy curtains.

He offered her an affectionate smile as he approached her. "How are you doing?"

"Why did you come up here?" she asked in wonderment.

"I needed to make sure you were okay. When you called me back and told me what was going on I was worried," he answered. He hugged her with one arm while placing a delicate kiss atop her head.

"It wasn't necessary," Jazmin said.

"Of course it was," he stated.

"I was simply calling you back Lamar, because you called me."

"And I felt like I needed to be here for you."

"Oh...well...that was sweet, but I told you Tanya was meeting me up here," she said. She glanced Tanya's way.

Tanya ignored Lamar's presence and looked at Jazmin. "Don't you need to be finding out about your man?"

Jazmin narrowed her eyes at Tanya for her rudeness. It didn't faze Tanya though.

Apologetically, Jazmin said to Lamar, "I appreciate you coming up here but I have a lot going on at the moment. So...you can leave and I'll talk with you later."

Lamar shot Tanya a hard look but softened when his eyes shifted back to Jazmin. "That's no problem, I guess. I was just trying to be here for you since the man you're pregnant by isn't here."

"Once again, I thank you," Jazmin said with more firmness and a rigid smile. "But I'm not in a really good mood. When I feel better, I'll call you."

"Is the baby fine?" Lamar asked.

Tanya groaned in an exaggerated dramatic manner, "Damn nigga! Didn't she just say she wasn't in a good mood, but you're still asking questions!"

"Tanya, I'm simply asking her if the baby is alright," Lamar said to her in an even controlled tone.

"What do you care?" Tanya asked. "It ain't your baby."

Choosing to ignore her, Lamar turned to Jazmin, "Make sure you call me later, okay?"

Jazmin nodded as someone entered the room again. This time it was the doctor stepping around the curtains.

The doctor glanced between Tanya and Lamar. He asked Jazmin, "I wanna talk to you about what's going on. Is it okay that these two remain in the room or would you like for them to leave?"

Tanya didn't give Jazmin an opportunity to answer. She got up saying, "Jazz, I'll be out here. You can discuss this privately. Whatever you want me to know, you'll tell me. C'mon, Lamar."

Jazmin found it odd that Lamar didn't budge. She looked at him. "I'll call you later."

Reluctance etched across Lamar's face, but he abided her wishes.

Once they were gone, the doctor pulled up on the little stool next to her. He began talking, "Ms. Foster, you are experiencing a miscarriage. Don't show any signs of why, but sometimes these things just happen. And in your case..."

———

After leaving the emergency room, it dawned on Jazmin that the reason she hadn't heard from Jah could be because he didn't know her number. He had never taken the time to memorize any of his programmed numbers in his phone. She was sure even Georgia hadn't heard from him. Jazmin's heart went out to her. The poor woman was dealing with so much at one time.

As she rushed to Desiree's house, Jazmin tried calling Abe but got no answer. The next best thing was to call Eli.

In such an annoyed and drawn out tone, Eli answered, "What do you want, Jazz? You don't never call me no more. You can't fuck with me since you got your own lil' baby now? Is that what it is?"

"Eli, shut up," Jazmin told him. "I need to know where your brother is. I can't reach him."

"He ain't here," Eli said smartly.

"Eli! C'mon, there's a situation I need for him to handle," she said desperately.

"Well, he's not even in the country right now. What kind of situation—hold on," he was saying. Jazmin could tell he pulled the phone away as she heard him shouting, "Avani! What have I told you about writing on people? You can't be doing that shit lil' girl. Not on your lil' brother...I don't care about them evil eyes you giving me. Kris, get your child..."

Lord, Jazmin thought. The mention of Avani's name made Jazmin smile. She used to babysit her often. Eli's daughter reminded her a lot of what Genesis would probably be like. Avani was something else. She looked at people with an indifferent gaze. And she was a little bully, a complete contrast to her parents.

Eli came back on the phone, "Okay, what was I saying?"

"The situation," Jazmin reminded him.

"Oh, yeah. What's going on?"

"Jah is locked up and I need someone that can get him out," she said.

"Locked up?" Eli questioned. He chuckled, "He aight. That's that nigga's second home. He comfortable."

"Eli!"

"You can't bail that nigga out?"

"It's not that easy. Georgia was explaining that with him being on parole they're not gonna let him go like that...And I need him out. Sheena just died. He can't miss her funeral. And I...I just need him out," she said overwhelmed with emotion.

Eli's tone changed to that of a serious one. "Damn. I didn't know that. When did Sheena die?"

"Like a few hours ago. That's when the police showed up and arrested him; talking about serious charges, like attempted murder. They showed no respect and didn't even care that him and his family were grieving."

"That's some fucked up shit. Let me call Lu and I'll call you back."

As the call ended, Jazmin was pulling in Desiree's driveway. She stayed in her car to call Georgia.

"Hello?"

"Hey, how's everything?" she asked.

"Just waiting. Jah hasn't called yet. It's been four hours now," Georgia said somberly.

"Well, I called my cousin and hopefully they can pull some strings."

"Strings? Did you not hear what that police said? That boy ain't getting out with no attempted murder."

"Abe and his daddy Luciano know people; for real Ms. Georgia," she assured her.

"We'll see. I mean, what was he doing with Sean anyway? Why would he try to kill him? Is it because of you?"

"I don't know what happened and we're not sure if Jah tried to kill him. But what I do find odd is Erica's name was mixed in it. Now that's weird..." she said as her voice trailed off. A thought came to her and she shook her head with pity. "I know Sean wasn't with Erica. This is just crazy."

"Wait a minute now. Say what? Sean was with Erica?"

"I guess. It makes sense," Jazmin said. "Look, as soon as I hear something back from Lu I'll call you so you'll know what's going on."

"Okay," Georgia said. "You be careful and — Wait. How did everything go at the emergency room? Is everything okay?"

"Uhm...I'll be fine," Jazmin answered sadly.

"You get you some rest and don't worry yourself with Jah's mess," Georgia told her.

"I'll try," she replied before ending the call.

Letting her head fall back on the headrest, she blew out a heavy breath of frustration. She wondered about Sean and Erica's present condition. Desiree should have some information.

Jazmin didn't get a chance to ring the doorbell because Damien swung the door open. He was heading out with a duffel bag and didn't offer her his usual smile. She could sense he was still uptight about everything that surfaced while they were in Gatlinburg.

"She's in the den," he muttered over his shoulder in passing.

She glanced back to see Damien heading for his car. She wondered what he was doing. She quickly made her way to Desiree's den.

9

Although Jazmin smiled at the sight of Genesis in Desiree's arms, the distressed look on Desiree's face gave her pause.

Taking a seat beside Desiree, Jazmin asked, "What's going on?"

Desiree sniffled. "He's leaving."

"Why? Because of the trip?"

Desiree nodded. "He's still mad. We got into an argument and he decided that it was best that he leave."

"Permanently? Y'all not getting a divorce, are yall?" asked Jazmin with genuine concern.

Desiree shrugged. She always knew that her past with Sean would catch up with her one day. She never considered that karma would mess up her world like this. She couldn't give Damien the baby he desired and now he didn't feel he could trust her.

Changing the subject, Jazmin asked, "How was 'lil fat mama?"

"She's a good baby; just a little demanding," Desiree chuckled. She shifted Genesis in her arms as a solemn look took over her face. She said to Jazmin, "I'm really sorry about what happened."

"I'm okay," Jazmin said to assure her. "Right now I'm just worried about Jah."

"I hope he can get out of this," Desiree said.

"Well, hopefully Lu can do something," Jazmin added.

Damien entered the den. His attitude was apparent, but he tried to show some concern. "How's Jah?"

Jazmin answered, "Don't know. No one has heard from him. I'm hoping Lu can work some magic and get him out though."

"Lu? As in Luciano Pavoni?" Damien asked.

"Yeah," she said.

Desiree turned up her nose and snarled, "What do you care?"

"Shut up, Dez," Damien snapped. "I'm not a selfish, uncaring individual, unlike you who only can think of herself."

"Why haven't you left yet?" she asked with a scowl. "Since you're leaving. Go ahead and leave!"

"I ain't got time for this shit," Damien mumbled under his breath. He looked at Jazmin, "If you can, can you update me when you've heard something about him?"

Jazmin nodded. "Sure."

She waited until Damien was out of sight again to whisper to her sister, "You're making it worse."

Desiree rolled her eyes. "I don't care. He's the one that's being silly. Everything that happened in the past was before he and I got married."

"I guess he felt like you should have told him about it."

Desiree uttered a noise in disbelief. "It was none of his business."

"But maybe it was something you should have disclosed when the doctor told you why you were having a hard time conceiving," Jazmin reasoned.

Desiree waved her hand dismissively. "Whatever Jazmin. You're talking as if you're not guilty of not disclosing information."

Jazmin didn't even want to go there. Instead, she asked, "So what about you and Rayven?"

"I tried reaching out to her. She doesn't want to talk to me anymore."

"If the whole Sean thing with you happened before they got together why is she so angry with you?"

In a meek voice, Desiree confessed, "Not the last incident. They were about to be married."

Jazmin winced at the bite of that information. "Damn, Dez."

Desiree gave Jazmin side eye. "You can't damn me, Jazz. You were with the man too, and thought Genni was his."

"Okay, but the difference is, I'm not Rayven's friend. Secondly, thinking had nothing to do with it. I *wanted* Genni to be his. As a matter of fact, I wanted Genni to be his so bad that I almost made a silly mistake. I'm glad I didn't."

"How do you feel about Jah trying to kill Sean?"

Jazmin shrugged. "I don't know what really happened. I would hope Jah wouldn't do something so stupid over nothing. But doesn't it seem strange to you that Erica and Sean were both attacked together?"

"Please don't tell me he was sleeping with her too! No wonder Jah flipped on them."

Damien stepped back into the den. "From what I heard that's a true statement."

"What did you hear?" Jazmin asked.

Desiree blew out a breath of frustration. "He's still here."

Ignoring Desiree, Damien explained, "Sean's been screwing Erica for years off and on. He basically passed her on to Jah but had Jah known Sean had her before him, I'm sure Jah wouldn't have went there with Erica."

13

"How do you know all of this?" Desiree asked.

Damien answered, "Straight from the horse's mouth."

Chapter 2

Rayven didn't know whether she was coming or going. Just as she was wrapping her mind around one issue, something else would pop up. Now, her no good husband had gotten into something else. She was less than thrilled when the authorities contacted her. She contemplated even going to see about him. But a part of her was curious about why he ended up in the hospital.

It wasn't until the next day that Rayven decided to visit her husband. After providing the staff with the special access code, Rayven was allowed to go to her husband's room. She figured the code was to keep unwanted visitors out, such as the person who probably wanted to finish what he started on Sean. *It deserves him right*, she thought.

She entered the room and was surprised to see there was a visitor already present.

Cautiously, Rayven slowly walked on the other side of Sean's hospital bed. She looked at Erica with question. Even more, Rayven was curious about Erica's bruises. They were nowhere near as damaging as Sean's, but they were obvious.

Rayven's presence didn't faze Erica at all.

"Why are you here?" Rayven asked.

"To see about Sean," Erica answered smartly.

Sean lifted his arm to quiet Erica. He looked at Rayven and tried to talk but his drug induced state along with the wires keeping his jaws in place made it hard for Rayven to understand him.

"What?" she asked. Then she peered at him closely. With a frown she asked, "Is your mouth wired shut?"

A unintellible noise came from Sean.

Ignoring him, Rayven glared at Erica. "Why is Sean your concern?"

"Ask him," Erica replied.

Rayven looked at Sean's bruised and battered body. Maybe she should be more focused on Sean and his condition, but of all people sitting in his room with him, why would it be Erica?

She asked Sean, "Why is she — you know what? Nevermind! You can't talk anyway. Do you know what happened to him?"

"The police didn't tell you?" Erica asked.

"They told me he was attacked and suffered some major injuries but nothing fatal."

"So why didn't you come up here yesterday when he almost didn't make it?" Erica asked.

"What do you mean almost didn't make it? When the police finally called me they said he was in stable condition."

"Well, he's been awake for a couple of hours now," Erica said. She looked at Sean and sneered, "And this the kind of wife you got? You were shot, jaw broken, ribs fractured and she didn't care."

"Hold on," Rayven objected. "You don't know me to be pointing out what kind of wife I am. What the hell are you doing up here anyway? Aren't you Jah's whore?"

"Bitch, I gotcho hoe," Erica said angrily.

Sean tried to say something but neither one of them was paying him much attention.

"Fuck you, and get out of my husband's room!" Rayven shot.

"Whatever," Erica said dismissively.

At this point Sean closed his eyes. The inevitable was sure to happen, and there wasn't a thing he could do to stop it; he couldn't even make up a lie to get out of it.

"I'll have security escort you out," Rayven said.

"Do what you feel like you gotta do," Erica said. "But before I go, I think you should know a couple of things."

"Yeah, I'm listening," Rayven crossed her arms across her chest in a guarded stance. She was preparing herself for whatever bullshit that was about to be spoken from Erica's mouth.

"Your husband and I have a son together. His name is DeSean and he's four, so that should let you know how long me and him been fucking," Erica answered proudly.

Sean let out a low groan. He hit the self-administering button for his pain medication.

Instead of reacting like she normally would, Rayven remained stoic in her bearings as she calmly told Erica, "Get out."

Erica hopped up with a satisfied smile. She looked at Sean. "I'll keep you updated about Jah."

The nurse that was heading in asked Erica, "You're leaving?"

Rayven heard Erica answer, "Oh, his wife is here now."

The nurse came in and looked at Rayven with an awkward stare. "Hello. I'm Laura, his daytime nurse. We were wondering when you were gonna make it up here."

Rayven wasn't really in a friendly mood. She let Laura do what she needed to do in the room and waited until she left.

When she looked down at Sean he was looking back at her through swollen lids. Although his eyes were open, it was evident he was miserable. But Rayven didn't care about the desperation or the apologies in his battered eyes.

She looked around to make sure no one would be coming into the room. In a quick movement she grabbed Sean by his jaw and squeezed as she spoke lowly and menacingly, "I'm so sick and tired of you! You have wronged me for the last time! Everything you get you fucking deserve!"

Sean tried to scream in response to the pain she caused but she covered his mouth with her other hand. He started kicking his legs languidly under the sheets. She ordered him to shut up before she let go.

Still whimpering, Sean tried to push the nurse button. Rayven slapped his hand away.

"No, you little punk," Rayven hissed. "You listen to me. I'm divorcing you and I will have full custody of our child. And you are paying me child support. By the time you leave here, your things will be out of my house. That's right, my house. Don't even think about coming by there. You can keep your car and live out of it for all I care. All this shit you're doing...making babies and sexing every female in sight, you got it buddy. But you won't be making a fool out of Rayven anymore. I'm done with you, Sean! And whoever done this to you should have killed you!"

————

So many things were running through Jah's mind. *Did he regret doing what he did to Sean and Erica?* Nope. If he could, he would do it all over again, only better. But that damn Erica, she was as foul as they came. He didn't shoot Sean. *Why would she lie on him like that?* Fortunately, the attempted murder charge didn't suffice; the DA charged him with another count of aggravated assault instead. The lawyer who appeared at his arraignment told him he had everything under control.

Then there was Juicy. He needed to know how she was doing. He didn't know what her stomach pains were about before the police hauled him off. One thing was for sure, his baby better be okay.

Snapping him out of his thoughts, Luciano asked him, "Where to, Jah?"

"To the condo," Jah told him. He said for what seemed like the millionth time, "Man, Lu, I 'preciate you coming through for a nigga, for real. I still don't know how you did it, but fuck it, I ain't gon worry 'bout it. A nigga out."

Lu looked at Jah with a wicked grin, "There was a glitch in the system."

"I bet the fuck it was knowing yo' ass," Jah chuckled. "You ain't even gotta tell me nothing else."

"Well, just so you know, I've got the best lawyer on the case," Luciano assured him. "Jackson is a phenomenal attorney."

"'Preciate that man," Jah mumbled.

Luciano leaned over and spoke to his driver. He provided him the address to Jah's condo.

"Listen, Jah, you stay put for a minute. Don't go anywhere near that man or that girl. We need you to stay out of trouble," Luciano spoke.

Jah nodded his acknowledgment of Luciano's words.

After another fifteen minutes, Jah arrived at his condo. He bid Luciano farewell with more expressed gratitude.

Letting himself in the condo, the smell of fried chicken hit his nostrils. He was beyond hungry and the aroma of food cooking only intensified his hunger.

Since the floorplan was open, Gina saw him as soon as he walked in. She smiled, wiping her hands on her dish towel. In her thick southern twang, she exclaimed, "Hey! You're out! How?"

Jah walked into the kitchen and plucked a drumstick from the batch of already fried chicken. Between bites he said, "I know peoples."

"What kind of people? Because those were some serious charges," Gina said.

"You being nosey now," he said as he walked away. "I 'on even know you like that to be tellin' you shit."

"I'll find out through Georgia," she said following behind him.

"My aunt ain't gon' tell you shit either," he said.

The pitter-patter of tiny feet approached them. Gina wore a big smile and stooped down with her arms widened to capture the little two year old.

"C'mere lil' man!" She crooned as she lifted him up into her arms. She pointed to Jah. "Look who's here!"

The little boy started giggling as he looked towards Jah, "Big head punk!"

Jah chuckled, "Yo' ass can't talk but you can say that shit."

"Caiden can talk," Gina said in her son's defense. She put him down. "Can't you lil' man?"

Caiden said, "I can talk. I three."

"You're not three just yet," Gina said. "It's coming though."

Caiden struggled to hold up his four fingers. "I five."

"Yo' son gon' be stupid," Jah laughed as he headed down the hall.

"You stupid!" Caiden yelled. "You not my daddy!"

Jah turned back around and looked at Caiden with amusement. "Where the fuck that come from? I know I ain't cho Daddy lil' nigga. But I still can whoop yo' ass."

"Nuh uh!" Caiden giggled.

Gina interrupted their play and told Caiden, "C'mon and wash your hands so you and Daddy can eat. Jah, do you want a full plate?"

Just as he was about to answer, Dewalis came down the hallway. "I thought I heard you. How in the hell did you get out?"

Despite their differences, Jah couldn't turn down his father's girlfriend Gina when she approached him about her financial hardships. She lost her apartment and was between jobs. Dewalis was having a hard time finding permanent employment. And since they couldn't afford childcare, they had to take turns caring for Caiden.

Once Sheena learned of Jah's *'private'* spot, she asked Jah to let Gina and Caiden stay at the condo. After all, Caiden was their little brother. *How could he turn his back on his little brother?*

Ignoring his father's inquiry, Jah asked, "Where's Sheena?"

"The coroner took her, Jah," Dewalis answered. He leaned up against the wall. "She couldn't stay in your auntie's house, you know that."

Jah's eyes lowered. He was devastated over his sister's death. He still couldn't believe she was gone.

"Me and your auntie are taking care of everything," Dewalis consoled. "The only thing you need to do is chill and stay out of trouble. Maybe spend some time with your daughter."

Jah shot him an angered look.

"What, Jah?" Dewalis asked defeated. "Say whatever it is you have to say."

"I ain't saying shit," Jah said in a gruff.

"No, we need to have this talk," Dewalis said. "Let's get this all out of the way cause every time you see me you wanna cuss me or fight me."

"I ain't put my hands on you now," Jah pointed out.

"But the way your face is all tightened, I can tell you want to," Dewalis said with a slight chuckle. "I'm guilty of every accusation you can throw at me. Why do you think I never fight back?"

"Cause I'll beatcho ass. Fuck you mean?" Jah stated.

The two men stood the same height and would have been an exact replica if it weren't for Jah's dreads and his thicker body. Despite that, Jah knew he could overpower his father any given day.

"If you say so," Dewalis said.

"When I said Gina and Caiden could stay, that didn't mean yo' ass too," Jah said.

"So what are we supposed to do? Live separate? I was staying with her and had nowhere to go my damn self."

"That ain't my problem," Jah said. He frowned and asked his father, "What the fuck you doing messing with her anyway? Got her pregnant and shit and can't even fuckin take care of her or yo' son. Hell, at least with me and Sheena, Mama was able to maintain on her own. Gina ain't nothing but twenty-two, nigga. You ain't shit, De."

"I'm looking for a job, Jah," he said.

"And in the meantime, yall mufuckas 'posed to live off me?"

25

"Not in that sense. I mean, just a lil' while…give us enough time to get on our feet."

"How old you is, De?"

"I'm fifty-two."

Jah shook his head in pity. "Ol' perverted ass nigga."

"How does that—"

Jah didn't want to hear Dewalis' argument. He cut him off, "I bet she thought you had her back too. So when Caiden get about five, eight… you gon' leave them too?"

"That's not my intentions."

Silence fell between them. Jah stared at his father intensely with his jaws clenching. Dewalis wore his most humble expression. And that was another thing that bothered Jah. He wasn't used to his father being such a passive man. This man before him, he didn't even know. So many years had passed since they were in either one's life consistently.

"If it wasn't for Caiden and Sheena, I woulda told y'all mufuckas no. But I'm gonna give you a lil' while," Jah said as he pivoted to head down the hallway.

Once in his bedroom, he sat on the edge of his bed. Releasing a discouraged breath, he fell back onto the bed and stared at the ceiling. He thanked God that he crossed paths with Abe Masters years ago. If he hadn't, he would be completely fucked. Jah considered himself lucky and very fortunate that he wasn't still sitting in jail. A person like him should have had a hold on his release due to his parole, but somehow, thanks to Luciano, it didn't flag him. However, he knew he still had to go through the whole process of a preliminary hearing and possibly a trial. He hoped Luciano really had his back because he couldn't see himself returning to prison again. He didn't want to leave his children like that.

Thoughts of his children prompted him to retrieve his phone from his pocket. It was dead. His charger was left at his aunt's house. He needed to know what Jazmin's pains were about before he got arrested. He hoped the baby was okay. Furthermore, he was missing his baby Genesis. The thought of not being able to hold her really got to him while he was in the criminal detention center. He needed to get his mind right, but he definitely had to see his baby.

———

The sight of blood every time she went to the bathroom worried Jazmin. She had been doing too much moving around and hadn't listened to any of the instructions her ER doctor had given her. Now, Dr. Bradshaw was telling her the same thing; stay in bed.

Caring for Genesis wouldn't allow her to stay in one place too long. It was times like this that she wished Jah was around. But if he were in her face at that moment, she would probably smack him.

Eli had called her earlier in the day to let her know that Luciano had gotten Jah out of jail. It had been a couple of days so she could understand that Jah was frustrated. However, it bothered her that Jah had yet to contact her. She was so impatient she called Georgia a couple of times, only to be told that Jah hadn't made contact with anyone.

"Hey, Jazz," Cassie said. Her face contorted with concern. "What's wrong?"

Jazmin crossed her bedroom floor to crawl back into bed. She sighed and somberly said, "Everything."

Cassie sympathized with her good friend. "It'll all work out."

Jazmin gave Cassie a look of suspicion. There was definitely a change in her. The aura about her was different. It was visible in this newfound glow to her cocoa brown face. Her sharply arched eyebrows rose trying to figure out why Jazmin was staring at her.

"What?" Cassie asked.

Jazmin said, "You've been acting really different lately."

Laughing guiltily, Cassie asked, "How is that?"

"You're nicer. You're optimistic, and you're not as hateful anymore. What's going on?" Jazmin teased.

"Hateful?" Cassie asked with feigned insult. "Me? I'm not hateful."

"You were. I'm seeing a change in you. Would it have something to do with Rock?" Jazmin grinned. "Have y'all been doing the nasty?"

Cassie scrunched her face up with disgust. "Eww! No!"

Jazmin stared at her hard until Cassie broke.

Laughing, Cassie said, "Okay, okay...maybe...something like that."

"Why are you so afraid to say it? I won't judge you, Cassie. I mean...look at all of the dumb things I've been doing. I'm not saying having feelings for Rock is dumb. He's alright."

"But he got two kids with two different women. And he ain't got no car!"

Jazmin snickered. "Why don't Rock have a car?"

"Because he wrecked his last one and his stupid ass let the insurance lapse," Cassie said as if she was annoyed.

"Oh yeah...I forgot about that. Well, you're his girl. You can drive him around," Jazmin joked.

"No I won't either," Cassie quickly retorted. She asked, "Is there anything you need me to do before I leave?"

"I don't think so," Jazmin said in thought. Genesis was sleep. She had taken her pain pill, and had something to drink. She was good.

"Well, call me if you need me," Cassie said. "I might come by tomorrow after I get off work."

"Okay," Jazmin said. She told her, "Can you lock the bottom lock when you leave."

Cassie got up and stretched. Jazmin eyed her friends figure. Cassie was an average, medium size, but she was never known for being shapely. However, Jazmin could see a hint of curves developing, especially around her hips.

Teasing, Jazmin said, "I see somebody getting a little thickness to themselves."

Cassie looked down at herself and waved Jazmin off. "You play too much."

Jazmin grinned, "Yeah. You know they say love be putting weight on you."

Cassie gave Jazmin a look of doubt. "Really?" Before walking out she said, "Let me know when you hear something about Jah."

After Cassie left, Jazmin lay in bed and listened to her television rather than actually watch it. Her mind wandered back to Jah. If he was guilty of the charges against him, she realized he would do time. Luciano was powerful, but there was no way Jah could just walk away free like that. Then again, she had no idea how the whole process worked. However, she had to question herself and what she truly wanted. *If Jah went back to prison, what future would she have with him? What kind of father could he be to Genesis behind bars?*

Jazmin groaned aloud. Jah always reacted to things instead of just thinking them through. Now, because of his impulsive behavior, he was possibly removing himself from her and Genesis' life. And that angered Jazmin. Furthermore, it bothered her that he hadn't even reached out to her.

Disobeying her doctor's orders, Jazmin hopped out of bed. She quickly got herself dressed and went downstairs to prepare Genesis' bag. Only when she was ready to walk out of the house did she disturb Genesis and get her together.

Heading towards Jah's condo, Jazmin felt anxious. She didn't know if he was going to be there, and if he was, she wasn't sure if he would have company. However, she needed to see him; she needed to make sure he was okay.

Once she got there she just sat in the car. She was afraid but didn't know exactly why. For some reason, she felt as if she no longer mattered to him. *If she did, why hadn't he bothered to come by to see her and Genesis? Why hadn't he called by now?*

After five more minutes of debating with herself, she decided to go in. She bypassed the attendant and went straight to the elevators. Seconds later she was knocking on Jah's door.

"Who the fuck is this?" Jah asked as he swung the door open. The annoyed scowl that was on his face immediately softened when he saw that it was Jazmin carrying Genesis in her carrier.

"Hey," she said meekly.

"Whatchu doing over here?" he asked.

"To see about you, obviously," she told him.

"Who told you I was out?"

"Eli." She was bothered by the fact that he had yet to invite her inside. He just stood inside the door. She asked, "Is this not a good time or something?"

He glanced behind him and answered dryly, "Really, it ain't."

Jazmin's eyes lowered as she willed herself not to be crushed. *Of all people, he wasn't happy to see her?*

"But I do wanna see my baby. I was gonna come by yo' house later," he told her.

"Just to see Genni?" she asked.

"You too, but shit…I kinda just wanna be to myself. Don't take the shit personal, Jazz," he tried to explain. "I'm just a lil' fucked up right now."

Her eyes watered. "But I'm your…"

When she hesitated, Jah asked, "My what?"

She shook her head as if it was no use. "Nevermind; forget I came."

Before she turned to walk away, Jah asked, "You gon' lemme come by later so I can spend some time with my baby?"

Jazmin gave it some thought. She was hurt that he wasn't exactly happy to see her, but it wasn't fair that she kept him from seeing Genesis.

As she was about to answer, the door opened wider behind Jah and a little grinning boy appeared. A woman's voice followed.

"Caiden! Get back here," called the woman.

Jazmin couldn't take her eyes away from the little boy, even as the woman scooped him up in her arms. He had a striking resemblance to Jah. It was undeniable.

The woman, the same woman that's always been at the condo smiled at Jazmin and said, "Oh, hey! You again."

"What you doin'?" Caiden asked.

Irritated, Jah said, "Y'all go on. Damn!"

"Is this Jazmin and baby Genesis?" the woman asked ignoring Jah's tone.

Wow, Jazmin thought. This woman knew about her but Jazmin didn't know about her. Jazmin let her eyes take in the woman fully. She was a petite but shapely woman. And her bright smile and eyes were getting on Jazmin's nerves. She appeared a little too happy for Jazmin's liking.

"Can y'all get the fuck on?" Jah said.

The woman giggled and looked at Jah apologetically, "Sorry. C'mon, Caiden; let's leave big head alone."

Jah pulled the door closed once they left. He looked back at Jazmin and asked again, "Can I see Genni?"

To say Jazmin was hurt and angry was an understatement. Reasoning and logic didn't present itself in her mind. The only thing she could think about was how Jah could have a child that he never told her about. On top of that, the child and the mother were there with him in his condo. Yet, here he was asking about Genesis.

"Fuck you, Jah," Jazmin spat. "You talk all that shit about me and Genni but you've been playing games all this time."

Genuinely confused, Jah asked, "What the fuck you talkin' 'bout?"

Jazmin sucked her teeth and dismissed him with a throw of her hand. She walked off hoping that he wouldn't try to stop her.

"Jazmin!" he called out to her.

She ignored him and pushed the elevator button repeatedly. Out of her peripheral vision she could see him approaching her.

"So you not gonna let me see Genni, and you just gon' leave like that?" Jah asked her.

The elevator dinged.

Jazmin turned to him and said as coldly as she could, "Once it's been determined that she's actually your child, then we'll see about visitation."

"What the fuck that mean?" he asked as he watched her step onto the elevator. "You on some mufuckin bullshit, Jazmin!"

Instead of replying to him she added, "Oh, by the way, I had a miscarriage but I'm sure you don't care."

As the doors closed, Jazmin was able to see the bewildered look on Jah's face.

All this time, she thought she meant something to Jah, even when she didn't want to see it. And now that she had gotten to a point where she realized that she wanted him just as much as he pretended to want her, this happened.

Chapter 3

Despite her pains and against her doctor's orders, Jazmin went to Sheena's funeral. There was no way she wouldn't be there. She had to show her support. Besides, she wanted to lay eyes on Jah.

After seeing him at the condo, she went home and cried. Once her uterine cramps returned she had to get herself together. She told herself she wouldn't obsess over it but she needed to see him with that girl. She had to be sure that what had developed between her and Jah was really over. It wasn't that she was ready to move on; she just didn't want to look like a fool for now wanting Jah when he didn't want her. In a way, the roles had been reversed.

"Who is that?" Desiree whispered next to her. "The girl beside Jah?"

They were seated several rows behind where Sheena's closest family sat. Where she and Desiree were, Jazmin had a good view of Jah. As Jazmin surveyed the scene, the girl from the condo was definitely present. She sat next to Jah and on the other side of her was Caiden. Beside the little boy was Jah's father.

37

"I don't know her name," Jazmin whispered back.

"Who is she?"

"I don't know," Jazmin shrugged her shoulders. "I guess she's Jah's girlfriend."

"Is that their son?" Desiree asked. "He looks just like him. I didn't know he had another baby mama."

Jazmin rolled her eyes upward. She turned to Desiree, "Will you be quiet?"

Desiree sat back for a second, and then she had the urge to look around. She was hoping Damien would show up. They really needed to talk. Instead of seeing her husband, she saw Tanya, Cassie, and Rock walking in.

"Your friends are here," Desiree whispered.

Jazmin could care less. Her attention was on that girl whispering something to Jah. From what she could see, Jah was emotional. He hadn't looked up at all. Whenever someone tried to speak to the family he wouldn't pay much attention to them. The only people Jazmin witnessed Jah speak to were her father, her cousin Abe, and Luciano. It was brief, like a quick nod or a couple of words. When she viewed Sheena's body, she turned to speak to the family and Jah blatantly ignored her.

Now it pissed Jazmin off that he was letting that girl whisper to him.

Jazmin's heart felt heavy. Despite whatever difference that existed between her and Jah now, it didn't stop her from being a compassionate person. Her heart went out to him and she hated to see him suffer. Maybe seeing Genesis would make him feel better, but she lay in Phyllis' arms, asleep. There was no way Jazmin wanted to disturb her. Genesis would have a fit and cause a lot of ruckus.

Jazmin tried to focus on the service. When Rita got up to sing the song Sheena specifically requested, Jah abruptly got up and headed out. Jazmin remembered Sheena stating that she wanted Stevie Wonder's *Never Dreamed You'd Leave in Summer* to be sung at her funeral. She was a big fan of Stevie Wonder and she loved that song. It was fitting, because she did leave everyone in the summer. Jazmin guessed it was too much for Jah to sit through.

Georgia as well as Dewalis quietly called after him. She watched Dewalis get up and hurry after him. Jazmin couldn't fight the urge so she hopped up and followed behind. Dewalis stopped at the church's door, inside the vestibule.

"Where did he go?" Jazmin asked.

Dewalis pointed towards the parking lot. "There's no talking to that boy right now."

Jazmin continued outside. He was almost at his car before Jazmin could call out to him.

"Jah!"

He ignored her. She half walked, half jogged towards him as he opened the car door to get in.

"Where you going?" Jazmin asked. She stood inside the door, preventing him from closing it. After seeing the scowl on his tear stained face, she thought maybe she should leave him alone. He was angry and hurt. She could empathize with him because she knew what it was like to lose a loved one.

Jah cut his eyes towards Jazmin. "Why, Jazz?"

"I just wanna make sure you're okay," she said.

He ignited the car and the engine came to life. "For what? You don't give a fuck 'bout me."

"That's a lie. I do care, despite how you treat me."

"How I treat you?" he was baffled.

She exhaled with frustration. "That's not even important right now. Are you okay, and why are you leaving?"

"Do it look like I'm fuckin okay!"

40

Jazmin didn't let his explosive tone waver her. He was hurting and she realized that. "I understand that—"

"Why the fuck do it matter?" he snapped.

"Cause clearly you're not okay and I don't want you—"

Losing his patience, he groaned. "Move out the way."

"Jah, what—"

"Jazmin," he interrupted her. He looked straight ahead and in a calm even tone said, "You getting on my mothafuckin' nerves."

"I'm just trying to make sure you—"

"Leave me the fuck alone!" he roared. "Goddamn! I just wanna be left the fuck alone."

Startled from his outburst, Jazmin stepped back. He didn't say anything else to her. He simply reached for his door and slammed it shut. If she had been a few inches closer to the car, he would have ran over her feet when he peeled off.

Jazmin stood there defeated as she watched his car disappear out of the church's parking lot. She knew he wasn't okay. No one ever knew what he was capable of when he was emotionally unstable. Sean's current condition was an example of that.

Jazmin headed back in the church. Paul was waiting for her at the entrance.

"Is he alright?"

Jazmin shrugged. "I don't know. He said he wanted to be left alone."

"Yeah, that much I heard," Paul said. He could see that his daughter was hurt by Jah's actions. He suggested, "Maybe he needs some space. He needs to clear his head. When he's ready, he'll come around. This is tough for him, Jazz."

"I know, but I'm trying to be there for him, Daddy," Jazmin said sadly.

"He knows. Just let him be for now. I'ma go in here and tell Abe to make sure he check on him though."

She sighed heavily, "Please do."

———

Jah lay on his back in Sheena's bed. While everyone was in his aunt's house eating and talking about stupid shit, he shut everyone out. People were getting on his nerves. The more they asked him how he was holding up, the more emotional he found himself getting. He just wanted to be left alone.

The only person that truly understood him was gone. After losing his mama, Sheena had always looked after him. She provided him a safety net when he felt no one else cared. She was his voice of reason and could open his eyes when he refused to see what was before him. She was the sweetest person he had ever encountered besides his mama. After getting to know Georgia more, Jah realized she was a sweet person too, but nothing like his mama and Sheena had been.

He always wanted a woman that reminded him of his mama. He used to think Jazmin was she. That's why he fell in love with her when they were kids. She appeared angelic, just as his mother had. Despite their weight, both women were beautiful in his eyes. Jazmin had a caring quality about her that he gravitated towards. The funny thing was, that even though he tried to express how he felt about her back then, she still reacted to him the same way she did now. She took his love for her as a joke.

Jah turned to the only companions he would allow in the room and said, "What the fuck is wrong with Juicy? Can y'all tell me?"

Mittenz and Sox raised their heads and looked at him.

"Y'all can't tell me?"

Mittenz lowered her head back down. Sox followed suit. They both lay on the bed beside Jah, looking just as sad as he felt.

"Fuck y'all then," he mumbled.

Sox raised her eyes at him then lowered them.

Damn, he thought. Sox and Mittenz were just as lost without Sheena as he was. Apologetically, Jah said, "I'm sorry."

He noticed how Sox and Mittenz were in a need of a nice grooming. "Damn, y'all looking kinda shabby. Uncle Jah gon' get y'all right."

There was a knock on the door.

"What the fuck!" he groaned out loud. "Leave me the fuck alone!"

The knock came again. There were several guesses as to who could be on the other side of the door. More than likely, he didn't want to be bothered with whoever it was.

The person knocked again. He got up and unlocked the door to allow the person in. He didn't wait to see who it was before returning to the bed.

Nivea stepped in, closing the door behind her.

Jah remained unmoved by her presence although he couldn't help but notice how her black wrap dress was hugging her hips and ass.

She eased onto the bed quietly. "When are you coming out of this room?"

"When I feel like it." His voice was flat.

"I don't think Sheena would want you doing this."

"Probably not," he said with a shrug.

"Have you ate anything?" she asked.

"I'm not hungry."

"Jah, you gotta eat something. Sheena would want you to eat. You know if she was here she would be shoving food down your throat right about now," she tried to joke.

Jah cut his eyes at her like she had said the dumbest shit he had ever heard. "If she was here, there would be no need for me to feel the way I do, dumb ass."

"Well damn, Jah! Excuse me for trying to care about your stubborn, hateful ass," she fussed.

"And this is why I don't wanna be fuckin' bothered," he told her.

"But you can't sit up in here and sulk either," she said.

Jah didn't respond to her.

She smiled, "How about you come over to my place to get away from all of this?"

"I don't wanna be—"

She cut him off. "I got something that may be able to take your mind off of all of this."

There she go, he thought. Nivea knew his heart belonged to Jazmin and she even acted as if she understood and wanted him happy with Jazmin. Yet, she always found a way to throw the pussy at him. Jah was beginning to think women were unstable beings. They didn't know what the hell they wanted from one day to the next.

"Pussy ain't gon' replace the fact that my sister is dead," he told her.

Nivea was taken aback. "Why do you always think that—?"

"Cause you do!" Jah interrupted her. "You might as well say, 'C'mon Jah, lemme put this pussy on you'. Shit, I ain't stupid, Niv."

She laughed and shook her head. "What's up with you and Jazmin?"

"Don't ask me about her," he answered.

"I saw her at the funeral but she hasn't come by here yet. I figured she would be in here comforting you."

"Well, she ain't." His thoughts went back to a few days ago when Jazmin showed up at the condo. One minute she was concerned about his wellbeing, then, the next she was snapping on him. And he didn't understand why she was talking about visitation and determining if Genesis was his. He didn't need a damn test to determine that. Genesis was his child. Period. But Jazmin wanted to be funny. He'd let her have that.

"Does that mean things are not working out for the two of you?" Nivea inquired.

"It means it ain't none of yo' business."

Nivea smiled. "I take that as a 'no'." Without warning, Nivea crawled over and straddled him.

Jah released a small laugh and shook his head.

Nivea teased, "Don't act like you don't need this."

Yes, he needed it. He just wasn't sure if he needed it from Nivea. She was cool to hang with and slide up in every now and then, but there was nothing deep there. He would prefer to be with someone he connected with and that understood him. That wasn't Nivea. She just wanted dick. And how he was feeling at the moment with her pussy mounted on his dick, he was in the mood to give it to her.

"Go on over to yo' house and I'll be over there," Jah told her as he playfully slapped her ass.

She leaned down and placed a kiss on his lips. Cockily, she smiled, "I knew you would change your mind."

———

Jazmin knew she should have went straight home and got back in bed but something wouldn't let her. After Sheena's burial people migrated to Georgia's house for the repast. Jazmin just wanted to spend a few minutes with the family. Let them know she came by and she would leave.

The driveway and streets were littered with parked cars. Jazmin actually squeezed in across the street between two cars. Just as she was about to open her door she saw Nivea coming out of Georgia's front door. She seemed to be in a hurry as she headed towards her house. Surprisingly, she didn't cross the yard. Jazmin watched as she walked around the side of Georgia's house. Nivea tapped on the window furthest back.

Jazmin's brows pinched with confusion as she watched Nivea reached out and pull back a white furball. Then what really made her mouth drop was seeing Jah climbing out of the window with another white furball.

She watched the two cross over to Nivea's property and disappear around the back of her house.

"Really, Jah?" Jazmin said aloud. He was no different from every other man. Jazmin was sure the other girl; his other baby mama, was inside and had no idea Jah had left.

Witnessing that turned Jazmin off. She no longer felt a desire to go inside. Instead, she drove off and headed home.

———

"Jazz, are you listening to me?" asked Tanya.

Jazmin hadn't meant to tune her friend out. Her mind kept drifting to Jah. She hadn't spoken to him or seen him since the funeral. Three days had passed since then. He pissed her off but she was still concerned about him. She wanted to know where his head was. Maybe this desire and need to speak to Jah was more than Jazmin being concerned. She missed him like crazy and was in need of his company. She wanted to be there for him right now. And she finally admitted to herself that she wanted to be the only woman to comfort him. However, he had options now. It hurt to know that she wasn't one of them.

With nothing else to do, Jazmin decided to actually listen to her doctor and get in bed and stay there. If her friends weren't calling to check on her, they were stopping by. Now Tanya was calling her for the fiftieth time that day.

"What did you say?" Jazmin asked.

"I said Tyrell's getting out soon," Tanya repeated.

Absently, Jazmin asked, "Who is Tyrell?"

Tanya blew air in frustration. "I swear to God if you wasn't my best friend! You haven't been listening to shit I've been saying."

"I'm sorry. It's just…" she let her words trail into a sigh.

"I know; you thinking about Jah. Call his ass!"

"No. I'm not gonna bother him."

"Well stop moping about him."

Jazmin blurted out what was weighing heaviest on her mind. "Did I push him away?"

"You want me to honestly answer that?"

"Yes. Did I?"

"You did," Tanya answered.

"But he got another baby mama," Jazmin tried to reason.

"What baby mama?"

"The girl that was at the funeral," she said. "With the little boy that look like him."

"Jazmin," Tanya said as she sighed. "You talking about that lil' bad ass boy that was at Georgia's house?"

"I don't know. I wasn't there."

"That lil' boy 'bout to be three years old. Think about it."

Jazmin didn't understand what she was supposed to be thinking about.

"Jazmin?"

"What?"

"When did Jah get out of prison?"

"Last year."

"How long was he there?"

Jazmin shrugged. "Five, six years."

"Do the math," Tanya told her.

Now that Tanya mentioned it, it didn't seem possible that Jah could have a child the age of the little boy. She said, "But don't they still do things in prison?"

"They don't get conjugal visits here."

"What about doing stuff on the low? I'm sure those guards get paid to look the other way."

Tanya laughed heartily. "You got a point there. But that don't sound like something Jah would do."

"If he want some bad enough I think any prisoner would jump on the opportunity," Jazmin joked.

"Seriously Jazz, that ain't Jah's lil' boy; that's his brother."

Jazmin sat up in her bed. "His what?"

"His brother. That's Dewalis' lil boy by that girl. Her name Gina."

"What?" Jazmin exclaimed in disbelief.

"If you would have come to Georgia's house after the funeral you would have learned that."

"I did come to Georgia's house," she said. She thought about seeing Jah and Nivea skipping over to her house. "I just didn't bother to go inside."

"Well, the girl is like thirty years younger than Dewalis' old ass. They've been staying at Jah's place cause they ain't had nowhere to go."

Jazmin couldn't believe what she was hearing. She had it all wrong. "Are you serious, Tanya?"

"Yeah. Hell, I was thinking the same thing; like why would she wanna be with Dewalis' ass."

"I ain't talking about her," Jazmin said. "Girl, I thought she was Jah's woman all this time. I got mad at him for nothing when I went over there. Damn!"

"You always doing Jah like that. Jazz, that's why he ain't there with you,"

"I don't always do him like that. You know Jah can be difficult."

"Yes you do. You don't give him the benefit of the doubt. It's like you subconsciously try to find something flawed about him to keep him away. That man loves you."

Jazmin smiled at the thought of Jah loving her. Then her smile faded when she thought of him and Nivea being together. "Not that much."

"Why? And don't say 'cause he ain't there with you and Genni. You tell Genni her daddy ain't there 'cause of her silly ass mama."

"Speaking of Genni and daddy; to be on the safe side, shouldn't I get them tested?"

"Who?"

"Jah and Sean."

"For what? Jazz, if you don't stop it! Anybody can see that Genni is Jah's baby."

"Yeah, but even Maury has proven that looks don't determine DNA," Jazmin pointed out.

"Do you really think there's a possibility that Sean could be Genni's daddy?"

Jazmin thought back on the time around her conception. She had sex with Jah that Saturday. The following Monday she had sex with Sean. That

Monday was her conception date, July 28th. She dismissed the idea of Jah being Genesis' daddy. She had dismissed the notion of them sleeping together completely. It had been something she didn't want to believe. At the time, she needed Genesis to be Sean's baby. It was what she foolishly thought would make him be with her solely.

"He could be," Jazmin finally said.

"Do you still want him to be?"

"No, not really. But I created enough mess with that whole situation. I just figured before things get any deeper that we all should know for sure."

"But Jah done signed the birth certificate. And he's convinced that Genni is his. Just leave well enough alone, Jazz."

"But what if...what if something happens and—"

"No, Jazz. Let Jah be her daddy and leave it alone. I'm serious."

Jazmin fell silent. She got what Tanya was saying but she still wanted to be sure.

Changing the subject, Jazmin said, "I think I need to go pay Sean and Rayven a visit. Woman to woman, I wanna clear the air with her."

Tanya released an impatient breath. "Lord Jesus."

"I need to do it for me, Tanya," Jazmin tried to explain.

"You just don't understand the phrase 'leave well enough alone', huh?"

Although Jazmin was laughing, she could hear someone ringing the doorbell. She frowned because she knew it wasn't Jah. He had a key and could just let himself in.

"Somebody is here," she told Tanya.

"Who is it?"

"I don't know. I'm about to find out. Don't hang up," Jazmin eased out of bed and made her way downstairs. She looked out of the peephole and groaned. For a moment, she contemplated whether she should open the door or not.

"Who is it?" Tanya asked.

"Mr. Worrisome," Jazmin answered. She said, "Let me call you back."

"Ugh! Yeah, call me back," Tanya said with disdain before hanging up.

Jazmin opened the door. In a dull voice she asked, "What are you doing here?"

"I came to check on you. You haven't been returning any of my calls or replying to my texts," Lamar said as he stepped inside the foyer.

Jazmin didn't recall actually inviting him in, which annoyed her even more.

She turned to face him. "I've been a little preoccupied these past few days."

"I gather that," Lamar said. He started walking towards the back.

Jazmin frowned and rolled her eyes. She followed him to her den.

"Where's the baby?" he asked.

"She's with my stepmama and daddy," Jazmin answered. She took a seat on her sofa.

Lamar smiled as he sat down beside her.

Unable to contain herself, Jazmin blurted out with irritation, "Okay, Lamar, why are you here?"

He chuckled, "To check on you."

"I'm fine," she told him.

"You don't seem like it. You seem bothered. You wanna talk about it?"

Jazmin couldn't help but to laugh. *Did he not realize he was the reason she seemed bothered at the moment?*

"What's funny?" he asked with a smile.

Jazmin gathered herself and shook her head. "Nothing."

"Have you given the idea of me and you anymore thought?" Lamar asked.

"No, actually, I haven't," she answered honestly.

Disappointment clouded his face. "So, you and Jah are working things out, huh?"

She shook her head and sighed. "No. We haven't really talked since the funeral."

Lamar seemed hopeful again. "Really? Has he shut you out or something?"

Jazmin shrugged.

"What about his charges?" Lamar asked.

She shrugged again. "I have no idea what's really going on with that."

"Wow, so he really isn't talking to you."

"Yeah, but I'ma give him his space."

Lamar cleared his throat uneasily before asking, "What are you prepared to do when he goes away to prison...*again*?"

"I hope he doesn't, but I've been thinking about that."

Sincerely, Lamar said, "Well, you know how I feel about Jah. You know how I feel about you. I feel like you deserve so much more than that. You certainly don't need to let life pass you by and dismiss a good man for a nigga that's always gonna be in and out of prison. Genni don't need it either."

Jazmin looked at Lamar intensely. Of course he wanted to paint Jah in a bad light; she got that. However, she couldn't help but to agree with him. *Why was she upset over an unstable, hot tempered, whorish criminal?* Lamar was right. She did deserve much more. More than she ever accepted from Sean and definitely more than what Jah was dishing out.

"Who's this good man that I'm dismissing?" Jazmin asked with a sneaky smile.

Lamar smiled brightly, "Me."

Chapter 4

Sean sat in his car contemplating if he should go inside or not. She had warned him about coming by, but he needed to talk to his wife. He knew she was fed up with him, but he had to try to make things work with Rayven. He was no longer delusional to the fact that he had fucked up. Everything, all of this was his fault. He owned up to that. He simply refused to believe that she was completely done with him. She had to have a little love left in her heart for him.

With his body still sore and recovering, he carefully made his way to the front door. His finger hovered over the doorbell as he debated over proceeding with this. *Fuck it*, he thought. The most she could do was tell him to leave and shut the door in his face. He pressed the doorbell.

Seconds later, Rayven swung the door open. She stood there, stone-faced, not impressed by his presence at all.

"Can I come in?" Sean asked. His mouth was still wired shut but he managed to master speaking with clarity.

Rayven didn't budge. "What do you want, Sean? None of your things are here. I made sure Ed grabbed everything."

"We need to talk," he said. Desperation gleamed in his eyes.

"No, we don't. I said all I needed to say when you were in the hospital."

Sean tried again. "Can I please come in?"

Rayven crossed her arms over her chest. "I don't think that's a good idea. Should you even be out and about? You still have some swelling in your face."

Sean was definitely in pain, but he'd rather be recovering at home; his home he shared with his wife.

Rayven looked around. "Who brought you here?"

"I drove," he said.

"You shouldn't be out," Rayven said showing a smidgen of sympathy. She studied his face and could tell he was miserable. The swelling of his eyes had gone down but a purple bruise still remained under each one. His posture was a telltale sign that his body was in pain. He was barely able to stand upright.

Giving in, she groaned, "Come on in."

Sean eased by her and stepped inside. Rayven closed the door behind her. She motioned with her hand for him to find his way to their family room.

"Can I get you anything?" she asked showing her hospitality.

"I'm fine," he said. He eased carefully onto the sofa.

Rayven sat on the loveseat and stared at him. She didn't know if she wanted to hate him or feel sorry for him.

"How's the baby?" Sean asked, breaking the silence between them.

"The baby is fine," With curiosity she asked, "Are you testifying against Jah?"

Sean shook his head.

"Good," she sneered. "Cause you deserved this. Sean, how could you do all of this to me and your friends?"

"I never meant for you to get hurt," he said. His eyes shifted away from her in remorse.

"So, you didn't think none of this would catch up to you eventually?"

"I wasn't thinking at all," he answered honestly. "I'm sorry."

Rayven fell silent.

Sean asked, "Can I come home?"

"And do what, Sean?" she asked in exasperation. "Do what? Work on our marriage?"

"Yes."

"How do you suppose we do that? Counseling? I don't think any amount of counseling could fix everything you've done."

"We could try."

"We could try," she echoed as if his words were absurd.

"For the baby," he added.

Rayven's head snapped in his direction so fast, Sean thought she had broken her neck.

"For the baby!" she bellowed angrily. "For the baby? Are you serious right now? Don't use this baby as a way back in. Were you thinking of this baby when you passed chlamydia on to me that you got from them nasty whores you messed around with? Were you thinking of this baby while you were going around thinking you were the father to another man's baby? Were you even thinking of this baby while you were with Erica and your son, DeSean? When have you ever thought of this baby? When, Sean!"

Sean didn't have an answer for any of those questions she slewed.

"Now come with something better, Sean," she told him.

"I love you," he said as he fought back tears.

"That ain't enough. Your love is worthless. It holds nothing." She wasn't moved at all by the tears.

Silence between them, but the sound of the doorbell sliced through it. Rayven got up and went to the door. *Could her day get any better?*

"What are you doing here?" she asked.

"I came by to talk to you," Jazmin said in a soft tone.

"We really don't have anything to talk about," Rayven said firmly.

"Of course we don't," Jazmin said sarcastically. She looked back at Sean's car and asked, "Is he here?"

"He is. You came to get him?"

Jazmin chuckled. "No. But I did need to speak to him too."

Rayven was about to tell Jazmin she would have to speak to Sean on her on time, but thought what the hell. Neither one of these people could hurt her any more than they already had. Rayven was developing a numbness to everybody.

She stepped aside and motioned for Jazmin to step inside. She pointed towards the back to direct Jazmin.

When Sean saw Jazmin appear, he didn't know what to think. His feelings for her were the same, but her being there at a time when he was trying to convince Rayven to take him back was not good timing.

Jazmin didn't bother walking any closer than necessary. This was the first time she had laid eyes on Sean since the whole incident. It had been two weeks but his injuries and bruises were still evident.

"Hey Sean," she said quietly.

"You don't wanna sit?" Rayven asked.

"It won't be necessary," Jazmin said. "I didn't plan to be here long."

Sean let his eyes roam her from head to toe. Jazmin was looking really good. Of course she was still thick but her curves were shaping up real nice. She seemed to have a fresh glow about her too. And her hair...he always loved her hair. She was wearing it all down flowing over her shoulders and down her back. It framed her oval shaped face just so. Jazmin was a very pretty woman. He didn't know why he could never see that in the past.

Jazmin looked at Rayven and began to speak. "Rayven, you're right. There's nothing at all for us to talk about. What I really should have said was I needed to tell you something. I don't expect for you to receive this with an open mind but for my own sanity and growth from this, I felt it was necessary that I apologize to you for my role in all of this. I'm sorry. Like I said, I know you won't accept it but I needed to say it."

"Why?" Rayven muttered.

Jazmin said, "Excuse me?"

Louder, Rayven repeated, "Why! Why did you do it?"

Jazmin pondered her reply. She finally said, "Giving you an explanation is almost like making an excuse for why I did it. And there is none. But think about it; my self-esteem isn't relevant in your life, is it? You could care less. It was wrong and I should have known better. That's all that it was; plain and simple. There's nothing to understand about why I did it either. How will those details help in you moving forward?"

Rayven gave it some thought. She mumbled, "I guess you have a point."

Jazmin looked at Sean. "And what I wanted to discuss with you is I would like to get a DNA test done. You know...just to make everything official."

Rayven started laughing quietly. Her giggles gradually grew into louder ones until she was laughing uncontrollably. Sean and Jazmin both looked at her fearing that she had gone mad.

"Don't they swab at the lab?" Rayven asked through giggles. "They can't swab his ass because his mouth is wired shut."

Astonished, Jazmin looked at Sean. Her mouth dropped open.

"Yeah Jah really kicked his ass," Rayven laughed.

"He broke your jaw?" Jazmin asked.

Sean rolled his eyes and sighed.

"Well, they'll just have to do it by blood," Jazmin said. She continued, "I just wanna make sure the right guy signed Genni's birth certificate."

Rayven turned to Sean and with humor asked, "Have you ever had DeSean tested?"

"DeSean?" Jazmin queried.

Rayven was delighted to say, "Oh yeah! I guess you didn't know but Sean was fucking Erica, Jah's little tramp. They have a four year old son together named DeSean. Jah caught them at Erica's house. That's why he kicked their asses."

Jazmin frowned as she looked at Sean. She shook her head pitying him. Her speculations were confirmed. She just couldn't believe it. "Erica?"

Sean didn't have a response. He diverted his eyes towards the television. During the brief silence between the three, footsteps could be heard upstairs.

Sean turned to Rayven with question.

Jazmin's eyes shifted to Rayven as well. She appeared a little apprehensive especially as the footsteps could be heard coming down the stairs.

"Ray! What are you laughing at down here?"

Jazmin peered around the corner to make sure she was hearing this voice right.

When his eyes landed on Jazmin, they doubled in size.

"J-J-Jazz-Jazmin, it's not what you think. Not at all," Damien stammered.

"Damien?" Sean questioned.

Damien's eyes shifted to Sean. He then looked at Rayven as if to ask why hadn't she warned him. Rayven could only offer him a guilty smirk.

"So this is why you left Desiree?" Jazmin asked.

"You hardly have any room to question his actions," Rayven pointed out.

"Oh shut up Rayven," Jazmin spat. She glared at Damien. "Tit for tat huh?"

"This is not that," Damien said in a desperate tone.

Jazmin shook her head. "Whatever Damien. If you wanna create an even bigger mess with all of this, go right ahead."

"I was only sleeping up there!" Damien exclaimed. "I wasn't doing anything—"

"Don't waste your time trying to convince me. Save that for Dez," Jazmin said. She headed back towards the living room to let herself out.

"Sleeping?" Sean asked for clarity.

"That's all," Damien said. "There's nothing going on between me and Rayven."

Sean stood up. He shot Rayven an angered look. He saw what she was doing. Rayven was set on making him hurt just as much as he hurt her. He understood it but he didn't like it.

"Where is your car?" Sean asked.

"It's in the garage," Rayven happily answered. She added, "You know, we were trying to be careful and didn't want no one being all in our business."

"Rayven!" Damien firmly said.

"It's cool," Sean said. He walked towards the living room. He could hear the two of them fussing.

Damien asked angrily, "Why would you do something like that?"

Before Sean pulled the door closed, Rayven yelled, "Because they deserve it!"

———

Jah was relieved and able to breathe once he walked out of court. His lawyer tried to have the case completely dismissed but the new assistant DA that was assigned to the case wasn't going for it. As far as she was concerned, Erica and Sean's cooperation was enough to pursue the case. Finding that the evidence was enough for Jah to have committed the crimes, the judge subsequently agreed.

Jackson explained to Jah that the new assistant DA was a by the book prosecutor. She didn't know of Luciano Pavoni as of yet and would likely not bend. Jah's best move was to convince Erica to stop showing up to court. She had made an appearance that day but disappeared quickly.

Nivea grabbed Jah's hand and gave him a comforting smile. "Everything is gonna work out bae."

"I hope the fuck so," he mumbled as they headed for Nivea's car.

"It will," she assured him.

Once inside the car Jah said, "Thank you for coming with me today."

"No problem," she said as she strapped herself in her seatbelt. Grabbing the steering wheel she asked, "Where to?"

"I'm hungry as hell," he said rubbing his stomach.

She chuckled, "I figure that. What do you have a taste for?" She added quickly, "Keep in mind I'm on the menu too."

"I'll pass," he mumbled with a hint of hilarity.

Nivea gave him a playful tap to his arm. "I don't know why you keep acting like you don't wanna taste."

"I thought we was talkin' 'bout mufuckin food."

"We are," she snickered. "I was just letting you know that I was an option too."

"That's dead," he said with finality.

"You kill me," she said with a roll of the eyes. "You act like it's such a disgusting thing to do."

"Eatin' pussy *is* disgusting," he chuckled at his obvious lie. He looked out the window and thought of the times he had feasted on Jazmin. Damn, he was missing her. Why did she have to be so fucking retarded?

"Whatever Jah. I know you do it. But what do you want to eat?"

When she started driving he said, "We can go anywhere; it don't fuckin' matter."

"How about Chipotle?"

"That's that Mexican shit ain't it?" he asked.

"Yep. You don't like Mexican?"

"It's aight. Just don't say shit when I blow up yo' bathroom," he said with a laugh.

"Really Jah?"

"I'm just warning yo ass."

She shook her head.

Jah took a second to admire Nivea. Over the past two weeks she had been there for him. Initially, like everyone else he tried to push her away. He had to give it to her though; she was insistent. No matter what, she wanted to be there for him unlike Jazmin. Although deep down inside Jah knew Nivea had her own motives, but for the time being he just rolled with it. Jazmin gave up easily; at least when it came to him. She always made assumptions and ran with them; not considering the idea of coming to him to discuss matters openly.

It wasn't that he wanted Jazmin to chase after him or even kiss his ass; but it felt good to know that he meant that much to someone. Sheena never gave up on him. She would bug him until he gave in. That's what Nivea had done and he had to admit, he had been enjoying her company on a different level; more than he had before. But she wasn't Jazmin. No matter what, that desire for Jazmin nagged at his every conscious thought. Time with Nivea was temporary though. Just something to hold him over to occupy his mind instead of being consumed with the sadness of his sister's death and the fact that Jazmin was so fucking retarded.

Jah asked, "When yo husband getting out?"

"In a couple of months," she answered.

"So in a couple of months, this shit between us gon' be over with?"

She glanced over at him. She quickly turned her attention back to the road. She answered, "It doesn't have to be."

"What the fuck that mean Niv?"

"It means me and Tee can be a thing of the past."

"So you sayin' you gon' break up wit that nigga to be with me?"

"Is that what you want Jah?"

He shook his head, "Nah, don't break up wit the nigga for me."

"But if you wanna pursue—"

Jah's phone interrupted her. After seeing who it was calling, he quickly answered it. "What up nigga?"

"I'm coming to get you so we can pay ol' girl a visit," Abe said.

"When cause I'm "bout to get something to eat. A mothafucka starving nigga."

"It'll be later around six; just be ready."

"Aight bet," Jah said.

"Bet," Abe said and disconnected the call.

Nivea asked, "Who was that?"

"Why you so mothafuckin nosey girl?" Jah questioned playfully.

"It was a quick call," she stated.

"You just focus yo ass on the road," he told her. His phone began ringing again. Thinking it was Abe calling back, he answered without paying attention to the caller ID.

"What nigga?" he answered.

"Nigga?"

Jah recognized the softness of her voice right away. His mood changed. He was thrilled to hear her voice, but he didn't want to come off as overzealous and in need of her attention. So he calmed his insides and put on a façade. Flatly he asked, "What the fuck you want?"

"I'm surprised you answered," Jazmin said.

73

"It was an accident. If I had known it was yo ass I sho in the fuck wouldn't have answered."

"Okay, what did I do to you Jah?" she asked.

"Naw nigga, we ain't chit-chatting. Get to the mothafuckin point."

"So I'm a nigga now?"

"What the fuck you want?" he pressed.

"I was calling to let you know I've already set it up for all of us to submit samples for the paternity test."

"I ain't going to that shit," he spat. Although he was thrilled that she called, he wasn't trying to listen to or discuss this matter with her. "I already told yo mufuckin ass; Genni my baby and that's all it is to it. Fuck outta here wit that bullshit Jazmin."

"Jah, don't you wanna know for certain?"

"What the fuck did I just say?" he asked growing agitated. "Getcho for certain ass off my mufuckin phone with that shit!"

"I know you better stop cussing me!" Jazmin shouted.

"Fuck you Jazmin," he told her. What was getting a paternity test going to prove? And what if he wasn't Genesis' biological father? Did she want to know just to have a real excuse to shut him out of her life completely?

"Don't you hang up either," she warned. "We need to talk Jah."

"No we don't. I'm done talkin to yo ass. It seem like the mo' we talk, the mo' stupid you get. I ain't got time for that shit or yo' mothafuckin can't make up yo mind ass. You know what Jazmin, I'm finally accepting that you don't give a fuck about me. You ain't never gave a fuck and I see you never will give a fuck. I'm done wit yo ass."

"Wait a minute Jah!" she yelled. "When I gave a fuck you pushed me away. I tried to be there for you when you got out of jail. I was the one that called to get in touch with Lu to get your ungrateful ass out. I came to the condo with Genni so that *we* could see you. You pushed me away then. I tried to—"

"Hol' up," he interrupted. "Yo stupid ass came over there talking crazy and flippin' out for no mothafuckin reason!"

"How many times are you going to call me stupid? Or dumb?" she asked offended. "Or you just don't have any respect for me now?"

Before Jah could respond, Nivea asked, "Who is that Jah?"

Jazmin said, "Oh! Now I see why you talkin' crazy. You know what Jah, don't come. We don't need you to be tested to know who Genni's daddy is. You do you!"

"I'ma do that any fuckin way."

"I hate you, I swear I do," Jazmin cried.

Again, Jah felt bad for hurting her feelings, but she had hurt his too many times. "Is that it? You wastin' my minutes."

Nivea snickered.

"What fuckin minutes!" Jazmin screamed. "You ain't got no fuckin minutes Jah!"

"To listen to this bullshit I do. I allow two mu'fuckin minutes a month for fuck shit. Them two mufuckas up. Get the fuck off my phone!" he rudely told her before ending the call.

———

Jazmin couldn't believe how that call just went down. It hurt her to the core. What made it worse was the fact that he was acting a fool in front of another female, likely Nivea.

After five minutes of crying, she picked up the phone and dialed another number.

"Hey sweetness," Lamar answered.

"You still wanna go out this weekend?" she asked through her sniffling.

"Of course," he said. She could hear the smile in his voice disappear when he asked, "Is everything okay?"

"Yeah," she told him.

"Are you sure? Are you crying?"

She fought back the cry building up in her throat. "I'm okay Lamar."

"Do I need to come over?" he asked with concern.

"No, you don't have to," she said. "I'll be alright. I'm just going through something."

"And I'm here Jazmin. I'll be over there when I get off from work. I'm not taking no for an answer either."

She managed a smile. "Okay."

"I love you and everything will be alright."

"Love you too," she whispered before ending the call.

A weird shiver coursed through her body. Telling Lamar she loved him didn't sit right. As a matter of fact, it felt very fake and forced. She cared for him but that was all. Who she truly loved was the person that made her heart race when they were on good terms and when they were on bad terms. She kept still just to notice how her heart pounded, face had tighten, and the rest of her body tensed. That damn Jah had an effect on her that she detested!

Looking at her phone she debated on whether she should send Jah a text message since talking to him was out of the question. She hit the message icon and her phone started ringing. *Speak of the devil*, she thought as she answered.

Jah cut her off, "One mo' goddamn thing...I'm getting Genni this weekend. I don't give a fuck about shit you gon say. I ain't seen my mufuckin baby in almost three weeks. You got me fucked up!"

"Fine," she told him defiantly. "I need a babysitter anyway."

"A babysitter? I ain't no fuckin' babysitter. Fuck you mean? Where the fuck you goin' any goddamn way? Goin' out with that punk ass sissy ass fuck nigga?"

"Don't worry about it," she said. "You come and get Genni Friday."

"You finna ride around in that lil gay ass red car wit that nigga?" Jah taunted.

She rolled her eyes at the amusement in his voice. "Why do you care? Worry about that bitch that's with you and your side nigga duties. Now you get the fuck off my phone!"

Victoriously she ended the call with a smile.

Chapter 5

Later that night, Jah ended up accompanying Abe as planned. Unable to find Erica at her place, Jah suggested that they pay her friend a visit. If anyone knew where Erica was or how to reach her, her friend would know Erica's whereabouts. She may not want to offer any information willingly, but Jah knew if the price was right she would sing.

"This where the bitch live?" Eli asked. His nose was turned up with disgust as he took in the sight of the house before them.

"Nigga stop actin' like you too good," Jah teased.

"Acting? I am too good," Eli stated.

From the passenger seat, Abe motioned for Eli to get out. "Go in there with him."

"The hell you say!" Eli exclaimed. "You see the way the house look. If it look like shit on the outside, I know it look and smell like shit on the inside."

"That's not always true," Abe chuckled.

Jah said, "With Kreature Kooler it is."

"See! I ain't going in there," Eli said adamantly.

"Just go in there," Abe ordered.

"You take your ass in there," Eli told him.

"I'm coming in a minute," Abe said.

Jah looked at Eli and snickered. "C'mon nigga. A lil dirt ain't gon' hurt you."

Eli looked as if he was about to have a fit. "Do I got to?"

"Get out!" Abe urged.

Reluctantly Eli got out of the SUV. He cut his eyes at his brother but followed Jah anyway.

When they got to the porch, the stench emitting from the house greeted them.

"Oh hell naw!" Eli said. "You smell that? I can't go in there!"

Jah grabbed Eli by the arm before he could walk away. "Naw lil nigga, you coming with me."

"Why? Why though?" Eli pressed.

"Because I don't need no shit behind this. This bitch might try to say I attacked or threatened her ug'lass too," Jah said. He opened the battered screen door and knocked on the dingy entry door.

Eli said, "Whatchu open the screen door for? Ain't no damn screen Jah! Just step through that shit."

"Shut up," Jah hissed.

Seconds later a little girl with her hair about her head came to the door. She asked, "Whatchu need?"

"What I need?" Jah asked with confusion.

Eli had covered his nose with his shirt. He could hear Abe cracking up in the truck. He shot his brother the middle finger.

"You buying something?" the little girl asked.

"What the fuck they selling out this shit?" Eli asked under his breath.

"Naw," Jah said to the girl. "Where Creature at?"

"Who dat Puddin'?" an older woman's voice asked.

The little girl stepped back with the door opened wider. The woman was sitting on the couch in the living room looking back at them. "Who is you?"

"I'm looking for Creature."

"Creature?" The woman was puzzled. She started laughing, "You must mean Creatia. Come on in."

Jah walked in but realized Eli wasn't moving. He reached back and grabbed Eli and pulled him along.

Immediately, Eli felt sick to his stomach and gagged. The stench was a lot stronger inside the house.

Jah looked over at Eli, "Stop that nigga."

"Fuck you!" Eli scowled.

"Yall can have a seat," the woman said.

"Uh uh," Eli uttered.

"That's aight. We'll stand," Jah said. He looked around the dirty living room and wondered how someone could live in these conditions. There was shit everywhere! And it wasn't that it was unorganized; it was just plain filthy.

"What the fuck! Do yall ever clean in this mufucka?" Jah asked angrily. He looked over by the window and noticed there was a baby in a playpen full of clothes.

"Now wait a minute now," the woman said defensively.

"Wait a minute my ass!" Jah was pissed. "You got kids up in this bitch living like this. This a mufuckin' hazard to every goddamn body up in here!"

Eli had a sudden sensation that something was crawling on him. He looked on his arm and noticed it was a waterbug. He flipped out as he shook it off of him. "Where the fuck this come from!"

Creatia came down the hallway. "What's going on...," Her words trailed off when she saw Jah. She spun on her heels and made a dash for her bedroom. Jah went after her. Eli followed behind him. The woman got up too.

When Eli got to the back of the house he realized he made a mistake. The living room was a better place to be. A grey cat sprinted by his feet. He wasn't sure if the cat was supposed to be grey or if it was that way because of how dirty the house was.

"What do you want Jah?" Creatia asked nervously. She hadn't been fast enough to shut the bedroom door.

"I wanna know why the fuck yall living like this witcho nasty ass," Jah asked.

"Fuck you Jah, okay," she said.

"Why yo lil' fat ass run for?" Jah asked.

"What's going on Creatia?" the woman asked. She was holding a worn broom in her hand.

Eli asked, "And what are you about to do with that broom?"

"Use it if I have to," the woman said with threat.

"If you have to?" Eli asked incredulously. "You need to! You can start with the living room! Hell, it don't look like you or anybody else in here have used one since the slaves started jumping them bitches!"

Jah asked, "Where's Erica?"

"Why?" Creatia asked.

"I need to talk to her," he said. He went to say something else but a big lump of clothes started moving on her bed. "The fuck!"

Eli was ready to sprint for the front door. Whatever was on that bed, Jah would have to face alone.

"Hey!" A groggy male's voice called from the bed. His head finally appeared. He was wearing a glower on his face because he was disturbed. "Why the fuck yall in here? Go head on with all that Creatia."

Before Creatia could reply, Jah said, "Ay nigga! How the fuck can yo ass sleep in this mothafuckin bed? Can't you see all this shit 'round yo ass?"

The man did a double take and fully woke from his slumber. Startled by the presence of Jah and Eli, he sat up. "Who the fuck is you niggas?"

"You got a roach in your afro sir," Eli told him.

The man didn't seem bothered. He looked to Creatia. "Who the hell is them?"

"Don't worry 'bout it Eli," Creatia said dismissively.

"Oh no the hell this nigga name ain't no damn Eli! I'm insulted," Eli said in disbelief. The sound of a dog's bark made Eli pause. "Is that a damn dog? In the house?"

The little girl said, "It's our dog Rocket."

"Why do po' folks always wanna have a damn dog?" Eli questioned no one in particular. He went on, "It's apparent yall can't take care of yourselves but you wanna bring fucking pets into the mix? Help me understand that."

"Why don't you shut yo smart mouf up!" the woman suggested aggressively.

"Why don't you go brush yo' teef!" Eli shot back.

Creatia motioned for everyone to back up. She said, "I'll talk to you Jah."

Pushing everyone back into the hallway caused Eli to step back into the bathroom. The horror slasher music played loudly in his head as he took in the sight of the horrid conditions of the bathroom. He started gagging all over again. He was traumatized and horrified. "Jesus, take me now!"

Creatia led Jah to the kitchen to talk to him privately. "What do you wanna know?"

"Where Erica?" Jah asked.

Eli found his way to the kitchen but immediately started heaving. It was so intense he was doubled over.

"What's wrong wit him?" the little girl asked.

Eli tried to point to the garbage can by the wall but he couldn't get control over his stomach.

Jah turned in the direction Eli was pointing. He got sick himself. "Aw hell naw!"

Angrily, Jah yelled, "Is that yo' fuckin' nigga in there? Get his mufuckin' ass up so he can take this goddamn trash out! Maggots every goddamn where! Can'tchu see that shit crawling!"

The door opened and in walked Abe. He turned right back around to leave back out. "Oh hell naw! I got kids to go home to. I can't be carrying no shit back to my home."

Eli hurried out of the house behind Abe. "Mothafucka! But you sent me in there."

"Your ass was stupid enough to stay in there," Abe said. "I ain't got nothing to do with that."

"Damn you Abe!" Eli shouted.

Abe hopped in the driver's seat of the SUV. "You and Jah walk home. Yall need to be quarantined or some shit."

"You bet not fuckin' leave me!"

Jah came outside and saw Abe backing out of the driveway. "Where that nigga going?"

"He leaving us," Eli said aggravated.

"Seriously?" Jah asked.

"I think I need a tetanus shot...some penicillin or something," Eli said. He looked pale and faint. "I think I just contracted hepatitis or something medical researchers or scientist or whoever the fuck deal with diseases have yet to discover."

Jah cut his eyes at Eli. He huffed, "I know Abe betta stop playin' and bring his ass back."

"There's a roach on your back," Eli told him. Images of the bathroom flashed in his mind and he started retching all over again.

———

Later the three men ended up at Southern Wild, a nightclub owned by BevyCo. Outside of club hours, it served as an elegant restaurant where fine southern cuisine was served. A live band played relaxing jazz music to add to the ambience. Patrons clinked their silverware against expensive dinnerware as they chatted amongst one another.

On a Tuesday night, the majority of people dining in there were privileged people who had nothing else better to do than to spend money. There were a few people there conducting business meetings, legit or criminal, over dinner.

They sat on a tiered level that gave them a perfect view of everyone in the place. Jah kept his eyes on the entrance. He was waiting on someone in particular.

"Jah, when you returning to work?" Abe asked.

"You need me back now?" Jah asked.

"No, you're good. I just wanted to make sure that was your intention."

"Nigga, what the fuck else am I gon do?"

"I just don't want you back out there in the streets," Abe said.

"I ain't tryna get out there like that no mo'," he said. "I love my freedom."

Eli said, "About damn time you realized that."

Jah cut his eyes at Eli and snarled, "Shut the fuck up nigga."

"I'm just sayin'," Eli shrugged. He took a sip of his drink.

With thought, Jah said, "I got my baby to think about now. It ain't just me no mo'."

"I can't believe you got a baby with my cousin," Eli turned up his nose and shook his head. "Why Jazz sleep with you? Of all people."

"Cause I'm that nigga!" Jah boasted.

"You *a* nigga. Just *a* nigga. Don't flatter yourself," Eli said with a roll of the eyes.

Jah focused on his hands in a nervous matter. He said, "But Jazz trippin and wanna get a DNA test."

"Why?" Abe asked. "She knows Genni is yours."

"Anybody can see that," Eli added. "Hell, even Lovely's blind ass can see that."

Jah laughed. He laughed harder at the look Abe gave his brother.

Eli tried to stifle his laughter as he looked at Abe innocently, "What?"

"Keep on making jokes at the expense of my wife," Abe said in a threatening tone.

"Abe, stop being so sensitive," Eli told him. "Lovely make fun of herself all the time."

"Yeah and you know why?" Abe asked.

"Why Abe?" Eli rolled his eyes.

"Keep on I'ma smack you," Abe warned.

Jah wanted Abe to get back to what he was saying. Yes, Jah found Eli's joking funny but truth was, Jah was fascinated by Lovely's impairment.

He has watched her in action and it amazed him because unless someone was informed, they would never know she couldn't see.

"Finish what you was sayin'," Jah urged.

In a serious tone, Abe said, "Making fun of herself is her way of dealing with it. It makes her less sensitive about the matter."

"Then why can't you do the same?" Eli asked.

Abe shook his head. "It's harder for me because...Do you know how heartbreaking it is for me to watch my kids go up to their mama and ask her to read them a book? And Lovely being the woman that she is don't let that stop her. She'll ask them what story it is and once they tell her, from memory she'll recite that book from beginning to end. She turn the pages when it's time and everything. And that fucks with me to witness that because I'm part of the reason she gotta do shit like that."

"You know what?" Eli said matter of factly. "I always thought she was making shit up."

"Shut the fuck up Eli," Abe cut his eyes at his brother.

Jah felt a pang of envy. He was jealous of Abe for having a woman in his life despite how they came to be; one that he cherished and loved the hell out of. That's what he wanted. Even more so now than before. Maybe it had something to do with losing his sister; he wasn't sure. But that desire was like a constant tug at his heart.

"Are you gonna do the DNA test?" Abe asked Jah snapping him out of his thoughts.

"I told her I wasn't doing it. I know Genni mine," Jah said.

"I guess she just wanna confirm it," Abe said. "Go ahead and do it."

Actually, Jah was afraid to do it. He wasn't really prepared to deal with it if the results proved that Sean was Genni's real father. He'd rather not know and just keep things the way they were.

"What if she ain't mine?" Jah asked lowly.

"That's what you're afraid of huh?" Abe asked.

"That's why I don't wanna do the shit," Jah said shaking his head.

"Look," Eli said. "Me and Abe done had our fair share of DNA testing. We also were hurt cause everybody seemed to be lying and keeping secrets. Even if you remain in Genni's life as her father, she still should know if Sean is her real daddy or not."

"You talking stupid," Jah said seriously. "I'm her real daddy. That's all there is to it."

"You a stubborn ass fucka," Eli said. "I hope Jazmin put your ass on child support too."

"Fuck you Eli," Jah said playfully.

Abe nodded towards the entrance. "Ay, your boy just arrived."

Jah looked towards the entrance. There was Rock, Ricky and Sean. Rock looked in their direction and acknowledged them with a head nod. He then led the other two up to where Abe, Eli and Jah sat.

Everyone exchanged greetings. They all were fine except Sean. He wasn't sure what was going on because he wasn't aware that Jah would be present, let alone accompanied by Abe and Eli.

"You aight nigga?" Jah asked once he noticed the apprehension on Sean's face.

"I'm cool," Sean said. "What's up?"

"Yo face," Eli winced. "That's what's up. Jah, I know you didn't do this to his face."

Jah chuckled while staring Sean down. "Yeah, that's my craftsmanship."

Rock tried not to laugh. "Nigga, you ain't right."

"Jaws still wired shut?" Jah asked menacingly.

"Damn, you fucked him up like that?" Eli asked with amazement. "I will always actively try not to get on your bad side. You and Abe need some type of anger classes or something."

"Shut up Eli," Abe ordered. He looked at Sean, "You know why you here?"

"Not really," Sean said carefully.

"This case against Jah," Abe said pointing to his friend. "We need for it to go away."

"I already said I wasn't testifying," Sean said nervously.

Eli said, "You could be a good ventriloquist. You said that really good without hardly moving your lips."

Rock laughed. "Man Eli, shut up!"

"We know you're not testifying," Abe said. "However, your girl ain't got the memo. She's cooperating with the DA."

"I told her not to," Sean said.

"She ain't gon listen to yo weak ass," Jah snarled with detest. "We need to find her ass and make sure she disappear."

"I don't know where—"

Sean was cut off by Abe. "Think about it before you let a lie come out of your mouth."

Sean looked defeated. He asked, "If she ain't at her friend's Creatia's house, then she at her sister's or cousin's house."

"Where they stay?" Jah asked.

"One stay in Cayce on Sixth. The cousin live on Georgia Court in Preston Taylor," Sean answered.

"You got an exact address?" Abe asked.

"Naw, but I can show you which units they stay in."

"Aight," Abe said getting up. "Yall ride with us."

"Wait," Eli objected. He guzzled down his drink. He asked, "Are we going in another person's dirty house? I don't think I can do it again Abe. That took a lot out of me today. And I feel like you should pay me some type of bonus or something."

Both Abe and Jah yelled, "Shut up Eli!"

———

Scratching her head, Erica felt herself becoming frustrated. "Yall need to get this shit up!"

"Stop yelling," her cousin Ronni said. "They just kids. They ain't hurtin' nothing."

"But they messing up yo house Ronni," Erica said. She sat down on the sofa.

"I don't mind," Ronni said. She took a pull from her cigarette. "They fine. Shit, let them play while they at peace."

Erica sighed. "I guess."

"Hell, this ain't shit compared to that nasty ass friend of yours. I can't believe you had my lil cousins over there like that," Ronni said angrily. "You know better than that Erica. You should've been brought yo' ass over here."

"Well I didn't know if you'd be cool with it," Erica said.

Ronni laughed. "You caught me at a good time. Me and Carlos broke up. He went back to his wife for now. But you best believe if he was still here then you would have to take yo' ass over Lisa's house."

Erica shook her head playfully. "You so ratchet."

"Not as ratchet as you," Ronni laughed.

There was a knock on the door. The two women exchanged alarmed looks. Erica got up and headed towards the kitchen while Ronni answered the door.

"Who is it?" Ronni demanded to know.

"Sean!"

Ronni unlocked the door and opened it. She asked, "What are you doing over here?"

"Where's Erica?" he asked.

Ronni was about to answer until a shadow caught her attention. She looked at Sean suspiciously, "Who's with you?"

"Nobody," Sean told her.

Ronni wasn't buying it. Sean didn't seem confident. She went to shut the door on him but was met with resistance. Before she knew it there were two other men pushing their way inside. She yelled, "Bitch run!"

That was Erica's que to make a dash for the back door. When she opened it she was greeted by none other than Jah.

Backing up with fear, she asked, "What do you want?"

Casually Jah said, "Just to talk."

Erica looked behind him and saw two more men step inside. "What yall plan on doing? Kill me?"

"You know what?" Abe asked with thought. "Your name alone makes me want to really do bad things to you. I can't stand that name. It's a derivative of Eric. I killed a nigga named Eric before. But fortunately for you, we're only here to talk."

Jah motioned for her to move towards the living room. Rock was standing over Ronni with his fist balled as if he was about to hit her.

"Bitch, say something else," Rock threatened.

"Yall need to get this nigga," Ronni said. "I don't know who he think he is but I ain't Erica."

"What that mean?" Ricky asked flatly. "You gon whoop all our asses in here? All of us? Every nigga standing in here six feet or better. Bitch, don't be stupid."

Eli looked around the space and nodded his head with approval. "Now this I can deal with. It's a lil ratchetto but it's clean. I can tell somebody sweep *and* mop up in here."

"Ratchetto?" Ronni asked offended. "Are you trying to say my place is ratchet and ghetto?"

"Crates aren't end tables boo boo," Eli taunted. "But I'll give you credit; at least you got a matching pair from Purity."

"Fuck you," Ronni mumbled.

A couple of kids made their way downstairs. The older one stared at the six strange men unsure of what to think. The younger one saw Sean and his face lit up.

"Daddy!"

Jah watched the little boy run over to Sean and hug his leg. There was no denying that the little boy was Sean's offspring.

"DeSean and Chubb, yall go back upstairs for a minute," Erica told the kids.

"But I wanna go with my daddy," DeSean whined.

"You'll go but not right now," Erica said. "Go on."

"Bye Daddy! I love you," DeSean called out before he ran upstairs behind the other boy.

Jah cut his eyes at Sean. He could tell he was struggling with how he related to the little boy. He couldn't even tell his son he loved him back. And that was not how Jah wanted things to be with him and Genni.

"Can yall get to it so yall can get the fuck out my house," Ronni griped.

"Can you shut the fuck up?" Rock retorted.

"Make me stupid ass," she countered.

Ignoring them, Jah said to Erica, "Don't pursue this court shit. They ain't got a case without you or Sean."

"I'll get in trouble," Erica said. "They subpoena me to everything."

"Fuck that shit," Jah told her. "Besides, you know I ain't do all that shit like you made it out to be. Why the fuck would you do that Erica?"

"So you didn't come into my house without my permission Jah? You didn't beat Sean to almost death? You didn't attack me and smack me? Who had their hand on the gun when the gun went off?"

"Man, you 'bout that bullshit," Jah grimaced. "I oughta smack yo retarded ass right now. Yo dusty ass kids let me in. You pulled that mothafuckin' gun out on me. The only fuckin' reason I touched that goddamn gun was to get it away from yo dumb ass. And because you wouldn't let go I smacked the shit outtayo black ass."

"Whatever Jah," Erica said dismissively.

Jah was about to leap on her until Abe stopped him. He shook his head to him. Abe turned to Erica. "How much?"

"How much what?" Erica asked.

"For you not to show up for court," Abe stated.

"Don't give her shit!" Jah objected.

Ronni said, "Twenty-five thousand!"

"And I'ma shove my size thirteen boot up yo ass twenty-five thousand times too," Abe shot.

Eli started snickering. He loved it. Ever since the ordeal with Lovely, Abe has been switching off and on. Before that he was always trying to do the right thing and conduct himself like the upstanding man he had come to be recognized as. Not anymore; Fyah was always lurking.

"Come again," Abe said.

"Five thousand," Erica said.

"Okay, let me explain how this is gonna work," Abe said. "Once you get your money you can't show up to any more court hearings. If you do, there won't be any offers like this one. Do you understand?"

Erica nodded.

Ronni sucked her teeth and rolled her eyes. "Bitch, you stupid. Five thousand ain't shit."

"Do you ever shut up?" Ricky asked.

"When can I get paid?" Erica wanted to know.

Abe gave it some thought. He answered, "June thirty-first."

Later in the SUV, after riding in silence, Rock finally asked, "Abe, you really gonna pay her when June thirty-first get here?"

Abe looked back at Rock on the third row. He looked at Jah, "Your friend stupid as hell."

Jah laughed. He turned to Rock. "Nigga, there ain't no mothafuckin June thirty-first. I didn't graduate high school but even I caught that shit."

"Aw!" Rock finally got it and started laughing at himself.

"Wait...what?" Ricky asked.

Eli shook his head, "Oh damn!"

Chapter 6

When Friday came, Jazmin wasn't surprised that Jah was insistent on still getting Genesis for the weekend. After all it was Father's Day the upcoming Sunday. She didn't give him any objections over the phone but when she saw him in person, she had planned to confront him about many things. She was disappointed when he didn't show up alone. He was with Nivea and her kids.

She told herself she wasn't going to let him get to her, but she couldn't downplay her attitude.

"So you're gonna throw her in my face every chance you get, huh?" she asked him.

Annoyed, Jah asked, "What the fuck you talkin' 'bout?"

"You and Nivea."

Jah waved her off dismissively. "Go head on with that bullshit Jazz. I didn't come here to get into it with yo stanky booty ass. I'm here for Genni and that's mothafuckin' it."

"Jah, what did I do to you?" Jazmin asked with vexation.

He ignored her and took Genesis' bag from her. "Just give me this shit so I can get the hell up outta here."

"I don't get you Jah," she said.

"That makes two of us then," he mumbled as he turned away from her.

She followed him to her front door. She didn't want to believe that their chances of being together were over. She didn't want to appear desperate only for him to take pleasure in rejecting her, but she felt compelled to beg him to stop all of this nonsense. It didn't make matters any better with him coming over looking scrumptious. He smelled wonderful too. She wanted to be wrapped in his arms and held tight. She wanted to touch his bare skin. She wanted a kiss. She wanted to be made love to.

"Jah," she called out to him.

He stopped at the door but didn't bother to look back at her. "What?"

"Can we stop this?"

"What is *this*?"

"This between us. The bickering and the attitudes."

Jah turned around and asked with amusement. "Did sissy dude cancel his date or somethin'?"

She shook her head. "No, we're going out tomorrow."

Jah didn't bother responding. He spun around and went out of the door.

"Jah!" she called.

She stood in her doorway and watched as he ignored her but proceeded to Nivea's car. Jazmin locked gazes with Nivea. The more the other woman smirked, the more Jazmin's insides boiled. What the hell had Nivea done to *her* Jah?

Jazmin stepped back into her house and slammed the door shut. She wanted to scream but instead she busied herself cleaning her already immaculate home. She had to do something to occupy her mind besides think of Jah.

Around seven that night the ladies came over. It was nothing major or planned; it just sort of ended up that way. Cassie, Tanya, Desiree and to Jazmin's surprise, Michelle.

Jazmin hadn't encounter Michelle since the cabin incident. She had been missing in action. Cassie took it upon herself to let Michelle tag along.

"Hey," Jazmin greeted the two ladies when they arrived.

Michelle responded cheerfully, "Hey."

Jazmin shot Cassie a look. Cassie gave Jazmin a look asking her to look over Michelle.

Jazmin would for the time being, but she wasn't in the mood to entertain mess for the night.

Tanya turned her nose up at the sight of Michelle as she stuffed her face with Oreos. Talking with her mouth full, she said, "Who went and got this bitch?"

"Whatever," Michelle said dismissively. She walked over and plucked a few cookies for herself. She looked at Tanya and turned up her nose. "Are you getting fatter?"

Tanya shot back, "I hope you choke on Sean's dick."

Michelle snickered. "You wish you could."

"Not on that sick shit," Tanya spat. "You the only one that still want his ass."

Before Michelle could respond, Desiree asked, "Sean's been with you Michelle?"

Michelle took a seat at the table. "Yep."

The other four women just stared at Michelle causing her to become uncomfortable. "What?" she asked innocently.

"What's wrong with you?" Tanya asked.

Michelle laughed haughtily. "Nothing. Why something gotta be wrong with me because I'm happier than all of you miserable bitches?"

"Something is wrong with you if you think you've won a prize," Desiree commented.

Michelle rolled her eyes dramatically and waved indifferently. "Anyway…I'm pregnant."

Tanya started laughing. "Please don't tell me by Sean."

"Are you?" Desiree wanted to know.

Michelle beamed proudly. "Yes I am."

Jazmin took a seat propping her elbow on the table to rest her face in the palm of her hand. She looked on at Michelle with empathy. "Poor thing."

"Don't poor thing me Miss Goody Two Shoes. You wanted Sean to be Genni's daddy so you're no better," Michelle sneered.

Aggravated, Tanya groaned, "Ugh! Who invited her?"

"I thought we all could catch up," Cassie spoke up. She cut her eyes at Michelle, "I didn't know she wanted to be messy."

Jazmin sighed, "She's not being messy. She's just the same Michelle she's always been. Arrogant and obnoxious."

Michelle let out a wry laugh. "Is that what you think of me Jazz?"

"It doesn't matter what I think of you. Keep doing you," Jazmin said sarcastically.

Tanya asked, "How far along are you?"

"I'm three months!" she said excitedly.

"Sean knows?" Desiree asked.

Michelle nodded. "Yeah, he knows. He's happy too."

"Happy?" Jazmin asked taken aback. "This man has a baby on the way by Rayven and he has a child with Erica. There's no telling how many more he have out there. He knows nothing about being a father; don't even seem like he's into kids but he's happy about your pregnancy?"

"A child with Erica? What!" they all exclaimed at once.

Jazmin giggled. "Yall didn't know about that either huh?"

"Why are you lying," Michelle asked.

"I'm not lying," Jazmin said. "Go ask your man. I'm so glad he didn't end up being Genni's daddy."

"Oh so you already did the test?" Desiree asked.

"No," Jazmin shook her head. "I just know deep down inside that Jah is Genni's daddy. But we're still getting tested."

Michelle laughed as if she had it all figured out. "Yall can't rob me of my joy. I don't care how you make Sean look; he's with me and that's all that matters."

Desiree shook her head pitying Michelle. "You wanted Sean for yourself and you got rid of everybody so yall can be this happily ever after couple with a baby. I hate to tell you, but you got the wrong guy."

"Oh like Damien turned out to be," Michelle said maliciously.

"What does Damien—?"

Michelle cut Desiree off. "Damien left you and he's at Rayven's now. And Jazz, Jah doesn't even want you. He's with Nivea. Tanya, nobody wants you. That's how it's always been and that's how it'll always be. The nigga that got you pregnant didn't even stick around because he was ashamed. And Cassie..."

Cassie's brow went up. She was ready to punch Michelle in the face.

Michelle grinned as she took pleasure in saying, "You know for a minute I was thinking this baby I'm carrying could be Rock's. But it's not. I'm sure it's Sean's."

"You fucked Rock?" Cassie asked in a disbelieving tone. "You knew where things were going between me and him."

"Well you was being stingy with the pussy. A man can only wait so long," Michelle said nonchalantly.

Before any of the other ladies could stop her, Cassie leaped over the table and had Michelle's throat in her hands.

"She's pregnant!" they tried to tell her while trying to pull Cassie off of Michelle.

"I don't care!" Cassie yelled. Tanya managed to pry her fingers from Michelle's neck.

Michelle got up with her purse hanging on her arm. She wore a silly smirk. "Aw! You must really like him."

"Fuck you hoe!" Cassie shouted angrily. "That's all you are. A trifling low life hoe who go around collecting everybody else's trash!"

Michelle looked around at all of the ladies. "Aren't we all?"

Jazmin finally said, "Michelle get out of my house. You need to go."

"I rode with Cassie," Michelle answered.

"Walk bitch!" Cassie spat.

Michelle scoffed with a laugh. "No problem. Maybe I'll call one of yall's men to come pick me up."

"Get out Michelle!" Desiree reiterated.

"Word of advice for all of yall miserable bitches," Michelle started as she headed out of the kitchen. "If you'd treat your men like they needed to be treated, you wouldn't push them into the arms of other bitches like me!"

Jazmin couldn't push Michelle out of her house fast enough. When she returned Cassie was on the phone going off on who she assumed was Rock. Tanya was trying to console Desiree.

"What's wrong?" Jazmin asked.

"Is she right?" Desiree asked through sniffles. "I mean, I didn't even give Damien a chance to talk to me when he came over."

"What did he say when he showed up?" Jazmin asked.

"A bunch of blah," Desiree stated. "I tuned him out. He got angry when he realized the locks had been changed."

"I bet," Tanya said.

"I wouldn't be surprised if Rayven was pregnant by Damien. He always wanted a baby anyway," Desiree hopelessly said. She asked, "Are we miserable bitches?"

Cassie's voice startled them, "I don't give a fuck about that Rock!"

Tanya returned to their conversation, "Tyrell wasn't ashamed of me. I don't know why she say shit like that. I mean he is getting out soon but I don't know where things between me and him really stand."

"How long has he been gone?" Jazmin asked. "Are we gonna ever get to meet him?"

"Yeah," Tanya said. "If he stay out of jail. He's been gone for two years this time."

"This time?" Desiree chuckled through her sorrows. "Yall and these jailbirds."

"And that was why I never took Jah seriously," Jazmin added with thought. She sighed. "He's always been in and out of correctional facilities for years. If he wasn't locked up he was running in the streets. I think this is the most stable he's been up until now. I'm so mad at him for doing what he did and not thinking about the repercussions of his actions. It's like, he's proving to be the bad guy everybody says he is."

"What's gonna happen if he have to do time behind this?" Desiree asked.

Jazmin shrugged. "I mean, I don't know. I have no intentions on dragging my baby to a filthy prison to see her father. And I don't wanna be bothered with a guy in prison either."

Tanya hummed deep in thought.

"What's that for?" Jazmin asked.

"I think Jah knows that," Tanya said. She added, "He knows you're not the type that will deal with that. He also knows Nivea can't commit to him either. Her husband will be getting out soon. I know this because she told me when we were at the cabin. Maybe he's keeping you at a distance because he knows he's gonna be gone again."

Jazmin pondered on Tanya's theory. Could that be it? Could that be why Jah was acting the way he was towards her? That possibility made her feel somewhat better. Jah could very well still love her but he too was afraid. Sometimes Jazmin forgot that Jah was human and capable of fearing being hurt.

Cassie ended her call and rejoined the ladies. She was infuriated. Without having to be questioned she started talking, "I mean what the fuck did I expect? Birds of a feather flock together. Right?"

"He admitted that he was with Michelle?" Tanya asked.

"No. He said she's lying but I don't believe his ass," Cassie said. Her phone started ringing. She silenced it and sent the caller to voicemail. Under her breath she said, "He can kiss my ass."

"Maybe he's telling the truth," Desiree said.

Cassie gave Desiree a look of doubt. "Rock is a hoe but I knew that. That's why I was hesitant to even get involved with him."

There was silence amongst the ladies. It was safe to say that Michelle was no longer a part of their circle.

Desiree got up and fetched her purse. "I need to talk to my husband."

"You're leaving?" Tanya asked.

"Yeah," Desiree nodded. She offered them a small smile as she said, "I'm pregnant."

Jazmin's mouth gaped open with surprise. "Really?"

Desiree didn't share the same excitement as her sister. She nodded sadly.

Concerned, Jazmin asked, "What's wrong? Aren't you happy about it?"

"I want to be but I'm not sure if this one will stick. I mean, I'd love for this to be a successful pregnancy."

"Have you told Damien?"

"No but I am now," Desiree said. She sighed with defeat. "I would really like for this pregnancy to be the one, but I don't know what's gonna become of me and Damien."

"Do you really think he got something going on with Rayven?" Jazmin asked.

"With everything that has transpired amongst all of us, why would I not think that?" Desiree pointed out.

"Yeah, you got a point. When I was there, Rayven just seemed really vindictive."

"Oh I know she's loving it. This is her revenge." Cassie said.

"Well, don't let it stress you Dez. Get plenty of rest and eat healthy." Jazmin told her.

Desiree offered her a small smile. "And don't tell anyone else ladies. I wanted to wait until I passed a safe point to tell anybody; at least fourteen weeks."

"How far along are you now?" Tanya asked.

"I'm six weeks and three days."

"Well congratulations," Tanya said as she stood up to hug Desiree. Cassie followed suit.

Jazmin walked around the kitchen table to give her sister a hug. When she pulled back she gave Desiree an assuring smile. "We'll get through these next eight weeks together."

Desiree smiled weakly. "Thanks Jazz. You're a good sister."

Jazmin smiled and gave Desiree another hug. It was a nice feeling finally being able to develop a loving relationship with her sister. It's something Jazmin would cherish.

———

Just as Jazmin stopped briefly to check herself in the mirror, her phone started ringing. She was hoping that it was Jah returning her call but that was wishful thinking. He knew how she was when Genni was away. She had to check on her baby every other hour of the day.

She scooped her phone off her bed grabbing her purse in the process. She glanced at the screen to see who was calling. She answered as she skipped downstairs.

"Hello?"

"How are you?"

"I'm good Sean. How are you?"

"Do you really care or are you just being nice?"

"Both," she chuckled.

"You don't hate me?" he asked.

"No. You know I'm not capable of doing that. I'm just disappointed in you Sean but we all have our share of shortcomings. I can't be any harder on you than I need to be on myself for the dumb decisions I've made."

"Yeah, but I dragged you into it all."

"I'm a grown woman. I knew what I was doing. But it's okay because I'm trying to move on past all of that. So what's up with the call?"

"The DNA testing; when do I have to go?"

"Once it's set up you can go by on your own time to give them a DNA sample. Me and Genni already did ours the other day."

"Is Jah giving his?"

"Jah is being stubborn right now. He's not doing it."

"What if...Jazz, what if Genesis is mine?"

"Then we'll go from there."

"It wouldn't change things between us?"

Jazmin knew where he was going with this; she would just play along for now. "What do you mean?"

"Do you still love me?"

She sighed. "Sean, I'll always love you. We got history as friends and history as lovers. I don't hate you."

"I still love you Jazz. I'm sorry I messed things up."

"All is forgiven."

"I wish Rayven could be like you," he said. "There's no getting through to her at all."

"Give her some time. She'll come around; especially when she have the baby."

"Oh she told me the baby wasn't mine," he told her.

"Really?"

"I think she's just trying to get back at me."

"Maybe so. Weren't you there that day to win her over?"

"Yeah and then you came."

Jazmin let out a soft giggle. "What does that mean?"

"When you showed up I realized I truly love you. I love you more than I love Rayven. But I know you love Jah."

"Yeah...well...Jah and I are not together like that. Hell, it might be for the best."

"I'm still here Jazmin."

"I know Sean," she said. Her doorbell rang. "Hey, I gotta go. Let me know when you've given your sample. The results are supposed to return like in three days."

"I will," he said. Before he hung up he said, "Don't forget Jazz, I love you."

Jazmin looked at her phone and smiled. It felt good to be more in control of her love life.

She answered the door and smiled. "Ready?"

"Yeah," Lamar beamed.

————

The following morning, Jazmin awakened in her bed in a good mood. She actually smiled as she did her morning bed stretch. She looked to the right of her and realized Lamar was still there. She expected him to slip off before she got up.

As she looked at the back of Lamar's bald head an image of dreads spread across her pillows flashed in her mind. She then thought of the times when she would look over and see a head with a nice low faded cut beside her. During those times, she remembered feeling the most excited. Every time Sean came over it made her day. Out of the three men, she was the most comfortable and most affectionate with him. If Sean were lying next to her in that moment, she would have thrown her arms around him and kissed him all over.

Lamar wasn't affectionate like that. And Jah…It wasn't that he was unaffectionate but she never allowed herself to become totally unguarded with him. She had to admit, she had been lousy to Jah. She was always quick to come to his defense whenever someone talked down on him but she would turn around and be skeptical of his intentions towards her.

If Jah were lying next to her, he would be pulling her on top of him for another round of sex. Just the thought of him made every woman part on her body ache. She was in need of that feeling but the idea of having sex made her nervous. After the miscarriage she didn't trust her body.

"Hey," she called out softly. She pushed Lamar gently. "I thought you had something to do this morning."

A fully clothed Lamar slowly stirred out of his slumber. He reached over to get his phone from the nightstand. Once he saw the time, he quickly hopped out of bed.

"Shit, I'm going to be late," he mumbled as he searched for his shoes.

Jazmin told him, "You took your shoes off downstairs."

Lamar hurried out of the room. Jazmin frowned as she hopped out of bed herself. She wondered what was so important that had him in a panic.

She came downstairs in time for him to pass her to get to the front door. "Lamar, slow down."

"I overslept," he told her. He was standing at the door. "I should have gone home last night."

"You were tired," she told him. "But I won't hold you up. Take care of your business and call me later."

He didn't even say goodbye or offer her a farewell kiss or hug before he rushed out the door. The way he was acting, she would think he had a wife to hurry home to. Of course it wasn't true. Lamar was still trying to make her his wife and put a baby in her. He talked about it the night before during their date. For some reason he felt as though Jazmin was about to be all his since things were not working out between her and Jah. She had to remind Lamar that she was still not ready to marry. She was still trying to sort out her feelings and figure out what she truly wanted.

And as usual, Lamar didn't bother to try to have sex with her last night. The most they did was some light kissing. It was rather disappointing.

Jazmin retrieved her phone and called her father. As soon as Paul answered, Jazmin sang into the phone, "Happy Father's Day Daddy!"

"Thank you baby girl," Paul replied. She could hear the smile in his voice.

"I'm coming by later," she told him.

"Come on! You know Phyllis is having a house full of people."

"I know. Have you spoke to Dez?"

"Actually she beat you this time," he chuckled.

Jazmin laughed. That was a first. Desiree was known for being self-centered and thinking of others as an afterthought. Usually the day would be almost over before she picked up the phone to wish someone a happy birthday or happy anniversary. Things were different for Desiree now. Jazmin assumed that everything that occurred over the past two months have put things in perspective for Desiree.

After Jazmin got off the phone with her father, she sent out a group text to all the fathers she knew wishing them all a Happy Father's Day. She left Jah out on purpose. She sent him one individually.

Jazmin: **Just wanted to say that I think you're a great father to Genni. From day 1 you've been there. Even if Genni turns out to be Sean's, you'll always be her Daddy. You're a good guy and I'm sorry for not appreciating you sooner. Happy Father's Day! I'm sorry for pushing you away...love you!**

She waited to see if he would respond. After five minutes the only texts she received were *Thank You*'s from all of the other guys she wished a Happy Father's Day to. None from Jah.

———

Rayven looked at herself in her bathroom's mirror. Her stomach seemed to be growing bigger by the minute. She was almost seven months. Lately, the idea of bringing a child into the world was the only thing that excited her. It was the only thing that she looked forward to. When she thought of her husband it soured her mood.

120

She hadn't made up her mind about how she would handle things with her and Sean. She hadn't even bothered to file for a divorce like she had threatened. The idea of getting back with him and trying to make their marriage work entered her mind from time to time. But thinking about the fact that he had so many extramarital relationships going on disgusted her. It wasn't easy to accept that her husband had slept with four women that she was fairly close to at some point or another.

She had gotten herself just about ready to leave when her doorbell sounded. She wondered who was visiting her on a Sunday afternoon. She went to the front door and looked through the peephole. What the fuck!

Rayven was thinking about opening the door when the person started beating on the door while ringing the doorbell. That made her mad enough to yank the door open.

"What!" Rayven bellowed angrily.

"Where's Sean?" Erica asked.

"He's not here!" Rayven returned. She looked down at the little boy beside Erica. Rayven didn't need to be told that the little boy was Sean's son, DeSean. He looked up at her with big innocent eyes.

Erica pushed DeSean forward. "When he get back tell him I said Happy Father's Day; he's all his."

Realizing what Erica was doing, Rayven objected, "No, no, no, no...We can't—"

Erica walked off the porch and hurried to the car sitting in the driveway. She opened the door and pulled out two half-full white garbage bags. She didn't even bother to bring them to Rayven; she just tossed them in the yard.

Rayven pulled DeSean by his hand and rushed towards the car. "Erica! You can't leave him here! Sean doesn't—"

Erica cut her off by hopping in the passenger seat and slamming the door. The driver hastily backed out of the driveway.

Defeated Rayven groaned. "This girl is crazy!"

DeSean looked up at her and quietly asked, "Can I see my daddy?"

Still in disbelief that Erica actually left her son with her, Rayven just stood there. She didn't know what to tell the little boy.

"Can I have something to eat?" DeSean asked.

Rayven looked down at DeSean. She couldn't be mean to him. It wasn't his fault he was born to an idiot mother and a deadbeat dad.

She retrieved the two trash bags one at a time and sat them in the living room. She didn't have anything quick to feed a kid in her home. She would just take him with her since she was on her way to her parents' house.

With her eyes still on DeSean, she dialed Sean's number. It went straight to voicemail. She tried again and got the same results.

She reached for DeSean's hand and said, "Okay, let's go get something to eat."

———

It was late when Jah returned Genni. Jazmin hadn't been in the house long before he was ringing her doorbell. When she opened the door she was disappointed to see he was with Nivea again. She was hoping she could talk to him before he left.

Jah didn't speak to her. He barely looked at her. Before he could walk out of the door, she stopped him.

"Did you get the text I sent earlier?" she asked.

"I got it," he mumbled.

"You couldn't respond?"

"I got distracted."

"A quick thank you would have been enough."

Jah rolled his eyes towards the door. Without looking at her he asked, "Is that it?"

"I wanted to talk to you," she told him.

He released a frustrated sigh. "I gotta go."

Jazmin grabbed his arm before he could exit. He looked at her hand on him and then at her. Normally, his scowl would make her uneasy but she didn't let it bother her this time.

"Can we be friends at least?" she asked desperately.

"We are," he said. He pulled away from her to make his exit.

Crushed, Jazmin simply shut the door.

———

How did he let his life go from sugar to shit? Sean went from having control to being controlled. He was at Rayven's mercy. He had lost Jazmin and wasn't sure if there was a possibility of hooking and reeling her back. If Genesis ended up being his, then maybe there was hope. He lost most of his homeboys. The only one that had anything to do with him was Ed.

He cut his eyes towards Michelle. Since Rayven had made it clear that he wasn't to return to their house, he had been staying with Michelle since he was discharged from the hospital. It wasn't where he wanted to be, but it would have to do for the time being. Michelle was getting the wrong idea though. She talked as if this arrangement was permanent.

"You're not trying to do anything today Sean?" Michelle asked.

Sean kept his eyes on the television and he shook his head.

"It's Father's Day," she told him. "My granny cooked dinner. You wanna go over there?"

"No."

"No," she echoed. She sat beside him on the sofa. "I got a question."

He looked towards her for her to continue.

"Why have you never said anything about the child you got with Erica?"

"Because he's nobody's business," Sean answered flatly.

"So you were just gonna keep him a secret?" she asked.

"Michelle, don't start with that," he warned.

Ignoring him she asked, "What about the baby I'm carrying?"

"What about it?"

"Is Rayven's baby the only one you'll claim?"

"Rayven's baby probably isn't mine," he answered.

"What is it? You just don't want kids at all or something?"

Sean didn't have an answer for her.

Michelle plastered a smile on her face. "Well, I'm having my baby."

Sean rolled his eyes.

She hopped up from the sofa. Before she walked off she tossed him his phone. "Yeah, Rayven's been calling you."

Angered, Sean asked, "You had my phone all this time?"

"Yeah," she said as she left the living room.

Sean returned Rayven's call.

"Hello?" There was a lot of noise in the background.

"You called me?" Sean asked.

"Yeah. Hold on," she told him.

A few seconds later, the background noise faded. Rayven said, "Your baby mama dropped your son off at the house."

"What?" he was shocked. "Why did she do that?"

"I don't know! All I know is she showed up, knocked on the door, pushed him to me, went back to the car and threw out two bags with his belongings in them."

Sean still wasn't understanding. "His belongings?"

"Yeah. His birth certificate, social security card, and shot records too. Is she not coming back for him?"

"The hell if I know," he said. "Where is he now?"

"He's with me of course. Did you think I would just leave him standing on the porch?"

"I don't know."

"I may hate you but I can't be mean to this child."

"Where are you?"

"I'm at my parents' house. He was hungry, really hungry. Do the girl feed him? He ate so much I thought his little stomach would burst. Right now he's playing around with the other kids over here."

"Okay." Sean didn't know what to think at the moment. Why would Erica just drop DeSean off like that?

"So when do you plan to come get him?" Rayven asked.

Sean looked around Michelle's little one bedroom apartment. He didn't even want to be there himself; bringing a child to have to care for there was the last thing he wanted to do.

"Can you...can he...just stay there with you?" Sean stammered.

"No, he can't," she replied. "I got work. You need to get him Sean."

"And do what with him?" he asked.

Rayven started laughing. "He's your son Sean. You take care of him. That's what being a parent is about."

"But...I...can't...," he was bewildered.

"Where are you Sean?" Rayven asked.

"I...uhm...I'm at Ed's," he lied.

Rayven didn't say anything.

"What else did Erica say when she dropped him off?" Sean asked.

"Nothing. She simply said that he was all yours and she left. She abandoned her child and didn't even bother to kiss him goodbye. He doesn't know that his mother has no intentions of coming back to get him any time soon. At the least, at the very least Sean, he could have his father. He's not my responsibility."

"You're still my wife," he said.

"That doesn't mean I have to be obligated to care for your child that you had with another woman," she countered.

"Let me come back home. I'm still healing. There's not enough room where I'm at. I'll be more comfortable trying to care for him there."

She didn't respond right away. He hoped that meant she was giving it some thought.

"Please Rayven," he pleaded.

Michelle walked into the living room and stared him down.

"I don't know Sean," Rayven said.

"Please."

Michelle said, "Why are you begging her? You don't need her—"

Sean covered up the phone and snapped, "I'm talking to my wife."

"So!" Michelle said boldly.

Sean glared at her as he returned to the phone. "Can I?"

"Who was that Sean?" Rayven asked.

"Nobody," he told her.

Rayven sighed. "Well, only because of DeSean, but I'll let you two stay here until you get better and can move on with him."

Sean smiled, "Thank you. Just tell me when to meet you."

"Okay," she said before ending the call.

Frowning Michelle stood there with her arms folded over her chest.

Sean smiled, "I'm going back home to my wife."

Chapter 7

Another holiday crept upon everyone and there was nothing more calming than the tranquility of a Saturday evening cruise in the vastness of Old Hickory Lake. It was an adults only gathering in celebration of the Fourth of July on a luxurious yacht thrown by none other than Luciano Pavoni. It would cruise the lake until it flowed into the Cumberland River leading them right to the riverfront in Nashville. There they would dock in time for the fireworks show at the Nissan Stadium.

"Bitch!" Tanya whispered excitedly. She held her eyes wide and mouth gaped open in awe as she took in the details of the oversized boat. "This shit look like a damn fancy hotel on water."

Jazmin giggled. "Shut up and act like you're used to something."

"But I ain't used to this," Tanya said. She surveyed the scene. There was about fifty people there in attendance with even more boarding, and because she knew Jazmin she was lucky to be one of them. A server walked by with a tray of champagne flutes filled with the bubbly pale colored liquid. Tanya grabbed two and offered one to Jazmin.

Jazmin shook her head. "No thanks."

Tanya shrugged and downed one of the flutes in one big gulp.

"Have you seen Cassie yet?" Jazmin asked.

"Uh uh," Tanya hummed. "But I seen Rock. All of them went down there." She pointed to the lower saloon.

"Is she still not talking to Rock?" Jazmin asked.

"I don't think so," Tanya told her. Looking out towards the land, she said, "I think I see her coming. Ain't that her in the red?"

Jazmin turned to look but her view was blocked by Lamar approaching her. He was wearing a smile and holding a drink in his hand.

"This is beyond amazing," he said. "Thanks for inviting me."

Jazmin smiled, "Isn't it nice?"

"Yes," he said. "I just walked the whole thing and it's like five levels altogether, six bedrooms total, a laundry room, and it even have a theater room. I could live on this boat without a care in the world."

"Could you operate it?" Jazmin asked in a teasing tone.

Lamar chuckled, "Probably not. I would have to have a crew."

"Are they about to undock?" Tanya asked.

Lamar answered, "I think they're giving a few more minutes. People are still arriving."

Tanya frowned. She had invited Tyriq's father. He told her he would come but he had yet to show up.

"I'll be back," Tanya said as she walked away.

Jazmin turned to Lamar and asked, "Do you plan to stay overnight?"

"Are you?" he asked.

Jazmin shrugged. "It depends. I know my cousins and their wives are. They always do."

"It would be nice," Lamar pondered.

Jazmin looked beyond Lamar and saw Jah. After seeing him with Nivea on his arm, she was glad she had invited Lamar. She would have hated to be there alone while Nivea walked around grinning in her face.

"Can you excuse me a minute," Jazmin said politely.

"Sure," Lamar said as he looked out towards the deck. "I see someone I know that I need to speak to anyway."

Jazmin didn't bothered to see who Lamar was talking about. She wanted to catch up with Jah before he disappeared back to the lower level. She approached him carefully.

"Hey," she greeted.

Jah looked at her but did a double take once he realized it was her before him. "What's up?"

A smile formed on her face. "What's up with that look you gave me?"

"Nothing," he said shaking his head. He asked, "Have you seen Ike? Abe want him."

"The last time I saw him, he was in the bridge with the guy driving this thing."

He looked at her from head to toe then toe to head. "You get prettied up for Noodle?"

"That is not his name Jah," she said. "And no, I got prettied up for the occasion."

"There's somethin' different 'bout you," he said. His eyes admired the contours of her shapely body. She was wearing a blue halter sundress that clung to her breasts, hips, and ass. She wore her hair parted in the middle with flowing loose curls. She had on more makeup than he was used to seeing her wear; but it was tasteful.

"Maybe because you haven't taken the time to actually look at me," she said. "You've been avoiding coming face to face with me. I'm not gonna ask you why but I'm glad you're actually talking to me right now."

"Yeah, we can put all that other shit behind us," he said.

Not understanding exactly what he meant, she threw out there for clarity, "So we're moving on, right?"

"Moving on from what?"

She shook her head with a light laugh. "Nothing Jah. So how are things with you and Nivea?"

"We good," was all he offered.

"You seem calmer. I guess she knows what it takes to settle you down."

"She aight," he said nonchalantly.

"Yall've grown closer. Are things — ?"

"Juicy, just ask me straight out what you wanna know. Stop beating around the mufuckin bush. Shit! You wanna know if her ass is my woman, just ask."

She blushed with embarrassment. "Okay Jah. Are yall an official couple?"

"None of yo goddamn business," he told her in a playful manner as he walked away from her.

Jazmin rolled her eyes. She really couldn't stand him.

———

"What's up man?" Lamar greeted his friend excitedly.

Landrus returned the same excitement. "Oh hey! What are you doing here?"

"I was invited by my lady friend," Lamar told him.

The woman with Landrus said, "Hey, I'm gonna go holla at Lovely and the other ladies."

"Okay," Landrus said after Jaci. He along with Lamar watched her as she switched away causing her curvaceous derriere to dance about in her dress.

Lamar turned back to Landrus with a teasing grin. "That's you huh?"

"Yeah and you were looking a lil too hard man," Landrus joked.

"She's fine though," Lamar told him.

"I know. She's the mother of my son."

"Oh that's her? Wow. I didn't expect that at all."

"That's my baby," Landrus said matter of factly. He then asked, "Ay, did you take care of that?"

"Yeah," Lamar nodded. "Thanks for coming through for me."

"No problem," Landrus told him. "So how are things now?"

"Well she was happy to get it over with," Lamar answered. "It was pretty hard watching her go through the whole process."

"Did she follow up with her gynecologist?"

"Oh yeah. She did everything you instructed. It wasn't that bad except for the pain she endured."

"Did you fill the prescription for the pain meds? They should have helped."

"Yeah," Lamar nodded. He noticed Jazmin approaching and got a little nervous.

Jazmin joined Lamar's side. "Hey Doctor Landrus. I just saw Jaci. I didn't know you two would be here."

"Yeah, Abe insisted. How have you been lil lady?"

Jazmin smiled, "I've been good." She looked between Landrus and Lamar and asked, "You two know each other?"

Lamar responded, "Yeah, we went to school together."

"Oh I forgot, you are old," Jazmin teased.

"Hey," Landrus warned playfully.

Jazmin asked, "How's the baby?"

"I was just about to ask you that," Landrus laughed. "Peanut's doing good. He's getting big so fast. It's like he wasn't a baby for long. How's

Genni? I saw her when Phyllis and your dad came to my parents' house one weekend."

"You did?" Jazmin beamed. "Isn't she big? She's always eating and fussing."

"She's gorgeous," Landrus said.

Proudly, Jazmin said, "Thank you." She looked up at Lamar and said, "If you need me I'm going down to the main saloon."

"Okay," Lamar said. He watched her walk away.

Landrus inquired, "She's your girl?"

Hesitantly, Lamar nodded.

"Damn. So was the...was it for Jazz? If I had known that I wouldn't have hooked you up with the pills. If her dad knew I assisted her with an abortion he would kill me," Landrus said.

"Nobody knows about it," Lamar assured him.

"Well that's good," Landrus said.

Changing the subject, Lamar asked, "So where you find your son's mother? She's not your everyday chick."

Landrus chuckled, "That's a long story."

———

Tanya was smiling from ear to ear. Tyrell had actually shown up. She didn't think he would make it. She was glad because now she could prove that Tyriq's daddy existed.

As Tanya made a few introductions, Jah glared in Tyrell's direction. Instantly he recognized Tyrell as someone he had many run-ins with while they both were housed in South Central Correctional Facility. Tyrell was grimy and not to be trusted. Those reasons alone were enough for Jah to not like his presence there.

Tyrell looked in Jah's direction and a wicked grin spread across his face. "'Sup nigga?"

Tanya asked, "You know Jah?"

"We was at South Central together," Jah answered keeping his eyes on Tyrell. This was supposed to be a nice enjoyable event. He didn't want to disappoint his friends who were there to have a good time and he ruin it for them, but he wanted to fuck Tyrell up on sight so bad. "Thickumz, how you know this fuck nigga?"

"This is Tyriq's daddy," she explained.

"Oh! He exists," Cassie boisterously exclaimed. "Hey, I'm Cassie one of Tanya's friends. We were beginning to think you didn't exist, but I guess you do."

Tanya smiled, "He does."

"You mean that snotty nose lil nigga is this mothafucka's son?" Jah asked in disbelief.

"Shut up Jah! You gon' leave my son alone," Tanya playfully cut her eyes at him.

No matter how much he teased Tanya, Jah still had mad love for her. He could tell that she was happy that Tyrell was there with her, but if Jah could have it his way he would put him off the boat.

"Ay, where can I get a drink?" Tyrell asked eyeing the glass in Jah's hand.

"It's some champagne right here," Tanya said pointing to a nearby server.

"Naw, not that shit," Tyrell said. "I want something stronger than that."

Ricky who was standing nearby said, "That's downstairs. Follow me and —"

Jah interrupted him, "Fuck that nigga. Don't show him shit."

Tanya frowned wondering why Jah would act that way.

Ricky chuckled, "Aight. Nigga you on yo own."

Once Jah and Ricky walked away, Tanya asked Tyrell, "Yall don't get along or something?"

"Fuck that bitch nigga," Tyrell said dismissively. He pushed Tanya forward with a scowl, "Move ya ass and take me to get a drink."

The goofy smile Cassie was wearing at first disappeared. If Jah didn't like Tyrell, then she knew to be wary of him. Furthermore, she didn't like how he just spoke to Tanya. Any other time Tanya would snap on a man for speaking to her like that and pushing on her, but Cassie could see that this was one of those situations where Tanya just appreciated any attention because of her self-esteem. Cassie didn't like it and she made a mental note to pull her friend aside later.

Jazmin had been enjoying herself so far. Seeing Jah and Nivea together wasn't as bad as before. Besides, Jah had yet to be still enough to pay Nivea much attention. Nivea spent a lot of time in the sky lounge sipping on sangria and chatting with a few other ladies.

Lamar seemed to be caught up in the excitement about the yacht and its luxurious amenities. He hadn't been paying her much attention either.

She stood on the lower level aft by the railing. She took in the scenery before her and enjoyed the cool breeze against her face. Amazingly, she didn't get sick like she thought she would have.

"Hey Jazz."

She looked over her shoulder and saw that Landrus had joined her by the rail. She smiled, "Hey. You see your woman trying to teach everybody how to twerk?"

Landrus scratched his head, "Uhm...yeah. She's gonna get enough of shaking her ass for everybody."

Jazmin laughed. "When are you two gonna get married?"

"Hmmm," he gave it some thought. He finally shrugged. "I don't know."

"Who's holding it up? You or her?"

"Well she doesn't mention it and I don't either."

"Just leave well enough alone huh?"

"Something like that."

She looked back out to the water. "I would love to be married one day."

"Lamar mentioned something about that."

Jazmin scrunched up her nose. "Not to him."

Landrus laughed. "Why not? Aren't you two happy?"

"He's just a friend to me. He wants more but I don't. He's asked me and I turned him down. He wants me to have a baby and I can't. I mean, I just had one."

Landrus' brow wrinkled with confusion. "A baby?"

"Yeah. He wanted me to have a baby, but at the time I was already pregnant," she explained.

"So why did you get an abortion?"

Now it was Jazmin's turn to look confused. "An abortion?"

"That's what I came over here to talk to you about. I just wanted to make sure that you don't tell anyone I'm the one that gave you the pills for it. If I had known it was for you, I probably would have told Lamar no."

Jazmin still couldn't understand what Landrus was talking about. "What are you talking about?"

"You didn't take the pills?" he asked.

"What pills? I had a miscarriage but not an abortion," she corrected.

"A miscarriage? When was this?"

"A month ago," she answered.

Landrus went into thought as did Jazmin. He asked her, "So you didn't want an abortion yet you somehow had a miscarriage?"

"An abortion never. Why do you think that?"

"Were you with Lamar a month ago?"

"Yes. It's when he proposed to me. I told him I couldn't. I was pregnant by someone else and my feelings for that person then were strong and they're still strong."

Suddenly, Landrus appeared bothered. It gave Jazmin reason to be concern. She asked, "What is it?"

"Did Lamar give you any medicine at all?"

"No," she said.

"Do you think he's capable of drugging you?"

"Drugging me? I don't understand why he would want to."

"Do you remember anytime around your miscarriage if he gave you something?"

Jazmin gave it some thought. "Well, right before I started miscarrying he had come over..." Her voice trailed as the reality hit her. She looked at Landrus and her eyes grew big in unbelieving discovery. "Oh my God!"

"Wait," Landrus tried to calm her down. He didn't want her going about it the wrong way causing a scene on the boat.

"What did he give me?" she demanded to know.

"Jazz, listen to me. I didn't know it was for you. He came to me and explain that he and his girl were in a situation and he wanted to handle it privately. You know what? I could lose my fuckin' license behind this shit."

Tears came to Jazmin's eyes, "I can't believe this."

"Don't cry Jazz," Landrus tried to comfort her.

"Oh my God," was all Jazmin could say.

Jah looked over and noticed Jazmin was upset. He wasn't supposed to care, but at the end of the day, Juicy was his heart no matter what. Not liking how she was being held by another man prompted him to go over to see what was going on.

"Juicy, what the fuck wrong with you?" Jah asked. He glared at Landrus. "What the fuck you do to her?"

"I didn't do anything," Landrus said. "She's just upset about something right now."

"This mothafucka do something to you?" Jah asked Jazmin.

"No Jah!" Jazmin cried. "He didn't do anything."

Jah ignored Jazmin. Glowering at Landrus, he asked, "Who the fuck you is anyway?"

"Hey, hey!" Abe rushed over interrupting. He pulled Jah by his arm before anything physical erupted between his two friends. "Calm your drunk ass down. No fighting today."

"Who the fuck is this Shaboo looking ass nigga?" Jah asked. "He making Juicy cry and shit. Ionlike that shit."

Eli, whose attention had turned to them started laughing. "Shaboo? It was *Shavoo* fool."

"Shavoo, Shaboo...who the fuck cares. It's that *Next Day Air* looking ass nigga," Jah barked while still glaring at Landrus.

"What's his problem?" Landrus asked Abe. "Clearly he doesn't know who I am."

"Mothafucka, who is you?" Jah snapped.

"Jah!" Abe spoke loudly to command his attention. "This is my close friend Dr. Landrus Goode. Landrus, this is my crazy ass friend Jah from back in my street days. Look over his ass; I'm in the process of reforming him."

"Fuck you Abe," Jah snarled. "Why I gotta be the crazy friend?"

"Cause you are," Eli told him.

"Hey," Jaci interrupted as she walked over. "Is everything okay over here?"

"Yeah," Landrus said pulling her close.

Jah's anger subsided quickly as he admired the shapeliness of Jaci's body. He said, "Damn! This you?"

"Really Jah?" Jazmin scolded.

"Are you alright nigga?" Abe asked Jah. He didn't give Jah a chance to answer. "Why don't you go sit your ass down somewhere? Drink some water or something."

"I ain't drunk," Jah said.

"Coulda fooled me," Jazmin said cutting her eyes at him.

Jah asked, "You okay Juicy?"

"I'm fine," she said. Jah's erratic behavior somehow made her temporarily forget about what she had just learned from Landrus.

"My bad nigga," Jah said to Landrus. He dapped him up. "This my Juicy and don't nobody fuck with her 'cept me."

Jazmin tried to suppress her smile. She had to admit, hearing him call her Juicy again felt really good.

"You aight," Landrus said. "Jazz is like a lil cousin to me."

Jaci teased, "Was Jah about to beat you up baby?"

"I was 'bout to throw that mufucka overboard," Jah boasted.

Eli started laughing. "Man, if you had done that! I would've died."

"Don't encourage him," Abe said to his brother. "Why don't you take your ass somewhere too?"

"Abe you don't want nobody having fun," Eli whined.

"Go have fun with your wife," Abe told him.

"Speaking of wives," Jaci said excitedly as she broke away from Landrus. "Abe, Lovely can twerk. I just taught her."

"How you teach her and she can't—" Eli was saying until Abe shot him a look. He whispered, "Nevermind."

Jaci said, "Did I mention she's drunk too? Come get your wife Abe."

Jazmin waited until she and Landrus were alone again to speak. She whispered, "Don't tell anybody, okay?"

"No, Lamar need to pay for what he did," Landrus said angrily.

"Well, I need to confirm that he really did it."

Landrus sucked his teeth in aggravation. "He did it! It makes sense Jazz. He did that shit and he needs to be dealt with."

"Just give me some time to confront him on it."

"Hell naw! I don't trust him after doing some shit like this."

"Landrus, you see how Jah just reacted to you? He will be a thousand times worse if he find out that Lamar was the cause of my miscarriage. After all, it was his baby that I lost."

"Him?"

"He's Genni's daddy too."

"Him?" Landrus asked again in disbelief.

"Yes, him. He already don't like Lamar. He'll kill him when he finds out. Just give me a minute."

Giving in, Landrus sighed. "Okay. Just promise that you don't try to confront Lamar on this by yourself."

"I won't," she said. She noticed Landrus looking past her. When she turned around it was Lamar. Before he could say anything, she told him on passing, "I'm not feeling too well. I think I'm gonna find a room to go lie down in."

"Okay," Lamar said. "Is there anything I can do for you?"

Jazmin shook her head as she walked away. *Sick bastard!*

Chapter 8

Nivea had been having a wonderful time. She loved the atmosphere, the array of food was great, the music, the laughter...she could get used to this crowd. The past couple of months spent with Jah had proven to be something she truly enjoyed. The only problem was her situation.

If she could get Jah to really commit to her, she wouldn't care about her husband. Things had been strained between them two for a long time anyway. Before he got locked up, their relationship was on rocky ground. It was his idea to get married. Nivea went along with it to prove to him that she was committed. But things changed. Her feelings for him weren't the same. And apparently his feelings for her weren't the same. They spoke on the phone discussing where things stood between them. Although she felt that she and Jah had something between them, she wasn't exactly confident in her answer.

That was another thing that was bothering her. He didn't speak much about her, but Nivea could see that Jah was still pining over Jazmin. His eyes spoke what his mouth wouldn't. Normally, Nivea would feel threatened but Jah seemed to be moving on from Jazmin. She had stepped back briefly to see where things were going between him and Jazmin. When she saw that nothing was happening, she got right back in line.

Just a little bit tipsy, Nivea decided to finally exit the sky lounge. She hadn't toured the whole boat but she had seen enough of it. She decided to head up to the sun deck where there were several people mingling. She was just about to join a few ladies at the table when she glanced over by the pool. Her heart did a flip flop and panic set in. *What the hell was he doing here?* He just so happen to look in her direction at the same time and their gazes locked.

She spun on her heels and headed down to the main deck where it was the liveliest. She looked over her shoulder and saw he was following her. She knew she couldn't get away from him without causing a scene so she decided to go to the bar to order a drink and play it smooth.

"Whatchu doing here?"

Nivea took her drink from the server and turned around to face her husband. "I should be asking you the same thing."

"Shit, I was invited. Who you here with?"

Nervously, she took a sip of her drink. Cutting her eyes she said to him, "I was invited by friends. So when were you gonna make it known that you were out Tee?"

"When the time came when I said I would be getting out," he answered. He looked at her suspiciously, "Why? You worried I was gonna catch yo ass doing some shit you ain't had no business doing?"

"No but why did you lie to me about your release?"

"I didn't. You saw what it said on the internet," he told her defensively. "Remember I told you to take care of that shit 'bout my time Niv and you acted like you didn't have time to do it. So I said fuck it and got my baby mama to take care of it. And guess what? After they did the calculations I ended up getting my sixty days credit. That's why I'm out right now. But you wouldn't care cause you don't give a fuck."

"Oh don't do that," Nivea shook her head while narrowing her eyes at him. "I did give a fuck…It was just too much."

"But you my wife. You supposed to handle things for me when I can't," he argued. His voice rose, "So who you here with?"

She glanced around hoping no one was paying them attention. "Friends," she answered.

She decided to throw it back on him. "Who you here with?"

"My baby mama," he told her. He looked across the saloon and saw his baby mama entering through the double doors. She didn't look too pleased. He nodded his head in her direction. "There she go. And I oughta get her to kick yo' ass."

Nivea looked in the direction he nodded. It was several women at the entrance. Women that she knew for a fact couldn't be his baby mama, let alone any woman that would have any dealings with him. "Who?"

Nivea got her answer when Tanya walked up to them with her brow pinched with question.

Tanya asked, "What's going on Ty?"

"Her?" Nivea asked with amusement.

"What the fuck you mean 'her'?" Tanya asked with an attitude.

Nivea scoffed, "This is your baby mama?"

"What's so fuckin' funny?" Tanya asked growing more agitated.

Already on alert, Tyrell quickly stepped in the middle to prevent Tanya from swinging on Nivea. She did manage to jab Nivea in the forehead. Nivea tried to move Tyrell out of the way so she could prove to Tanya that she wasn't scared of her. Both women tried their best to get to the other. At this point everyone in the main saloon was focused on them.

"Tanya!" Tyrell shouted as he pushed her back. "Calm your ass down!"

"I'm tryna figure out what the fuck is so goddamn funny!" Tanya yelled ferociously. "You fuckin slut hoe!"

"Whatever you fat bitch!" Nivea retorted.

Cassie came to Tanya's aide. "What's going on? Why this bitch tripping?"

"That's what the fuck I'm tryna figure out," Tanya said glaring at Nivea.

Nivea looked at Tyrell and said, "Tell her who I am Tee."

"Who is she *Tee*?" Tanya asked mockingly.

"She my wife," Tyrell answered.

"This bitch?" Tanya asked. Now it was time for her to be amused. "This the bitch you married huh?"

"Yeah fat ass. I'm the wife, so back the fuck up and know your place."

Tanya went for her again. Cassie joined her making it almost impossible for Tyrell to control them both. Rock tried to contain Cassie but she ended up swinging on him. She hit him dead on the nose.

"Fuck!" Rock released Cassie and held his nose. In doing so, Cassie charged right back for Nivea. Tanya was able to exchange harsh words with Tyrell while Cassie handled the ass whooping on Nivea.

Caught up in the moment, Nivea never gave much thought to Jah and how he felt about the way she was acting or the fact that her husband was there. She continued to taunt Tanya and Cassie both while a few others along with Tyrell tried to defuse the situation.

There was no place for Jah in any of the argument. He remained neutral. What was happening before him was Nivea's shit. With Tyrell up in the mix, Jah didn't want any parts of it.

Nivea finally glanced Jah's way. He shook his head like she disgusted him. Surprisingly, he didn't feel a need to say anything, which bothered her. He dipped around the corner heading to the main level lobby.

"C'mon Nivea," Tyrell ordered grabbing her by the arm in a forceful manner. "Lemme holla at you. Tanya, I'll be back."

Tanya stood there with her mouth hung open as she watched Tyrell walk off pulling Nivea along with him.

"Ain't that a bitch!" Tanya grumbled out loud.

Cassie shook her head, "Jah know that nigga her husband?"

"I don't think so," Tanya said. Of all people to be Tyrell's wife, Nivea's ass had to be her! And considering the fact that Jah wasn't liking Tyrell and he was fucking his wife; this wasn't good.

––––––––

Tyrell called himself pulling Nivea off somewhere private, but they ended up right in front of Jah. He watched them as they argued. Nivea seemed to stand her ground but her body language told Jah she was afraid of Tyrell.

Tyrell said his final words before leaving Nivea looking distraught and hurt. She looked up and made eye contact with Jah.

Before she could call out to him, Jah made his way to the lower deck. He didn't have to look back to know that Nivea had followed him.

"Jah, wait a minute," Nivea called out to him. She caught up with him right outside the first guest cabin.

"Take yo' ass back up there to yo husband," Jah told her. "You all proud and shit rubbin it in Thickumz's face. That nigga ain't respecting neither one of yall but you want every mothafucka to know he yo husband though."

"It ain't like that," she tried to explain. "I didn't know he was here."

"How you manage not to see his ass? That don't even make mufuckin' sense."

She shrugged. "I've been on the middle level all day. I'm just now walking around."

"Why you follow me down here?"

"Because I wanna make sure we're cool," she said.

"I ain't fuckin' with you no' mo'. You that nigga gal. If I had known that, I wouldn't've never fucked witcho ass like that in the first mothafuckin' place."

"Well it's too late for all that."

"The fuck you mean?" Jah spat. "Anything that got to do wit that nigga, I want no parts of. You got that shit Niv. All of it."

Nivea could see that his disinterest in her was growing.

"C'mon Jah," she pleaded. "All of this can be worked out and looked over."

Annoyed, he reached for the knob of the cabin and said, "I gotta take a piss."

"Can I come in with you?" she asked.

"No," he told her as he opened the door. "I'll holla atchu later."

She just stood there as he backed into the room. With the door still open, Jah motioned with his hand for her to leave. "Take yo ass on fo' he come down here looking fo' you and I have to beat his ass."

She rolled her eyes dramatically and blew out a breath of frustration before turning to leave.

Jah closed the door and was about to head to the ensuite bathroom when the sight of Jazmin sitting on the bed caught him by surprise.

His face contorted in his infamous scowl. "What the fuck you doin in here?"

"I was already in here lying in bed," she explained with a sniffle.

"Well get the fuck out," he told her proceeding to the bathroom.

Jazmin frowned. She tried to speak above the sound of his urine streaming into the toilet. "How are you gonna tell me to get out? I was in here first."

When Jah was finished handling his business, he came back in the room and asked, "What the fuck you say?"

"I said I was here first. Abe said I can have this room. The other three rooms down here aren't occupied yet. Go in one of those."

"So," was all he said. He scooped up the remote to the wall encased television and sat at the foot of the bed.

Jazmin groaned with exasperation. "C'mon Jah. I really don't feel like being bothered."

He ignored her and continued to channel surf.

She scooted to the edge of the bed. In a huff she said, "I'll just go to another room."

"You ain't gotta go," he said getting up. He tossed the remote back on the bed. Jah's eyes traveled the length of her body. There was something about how voluptuous she was that had him salivating ever since he first encountered her earlier that day. He tried avoiding her but somehow she would end up wherever he was on the boat. He couldn't keep his eyes off of her. He admired the thickness of her and how she was sculpted with curves that truly represented a real woman's body.

Then there was the beauty of her face that shone brilliantly whenever she smiled. But at the moment he noticed that the brightness she possessed earlier was missing. For the first time he noticed she had been crying.

Concerned he asked, "What the fuck wrong wit you?"

"I wasn't feeling good so I came to lay down for a little while," she answered. She swung both her legs onto the bed and sat up against the headboard of the bed.

"What's wrong wit you?" he asked again.

"Just a lil nauseous," she said quietly.

Jah turned around to look at her. "Why you nauseous? You pregnant again?"

Jazmin frowned. "Again? No, Jah."

Jah chuckled, "Ol' boy still ain't hit that huh?"

"How did me being nauseous lead to Lamar?"

"You ain't gon answer the question?"

Jazmin sucked her teeth as if she was annoyed. "Lamar and I are friends. That's it. Nothing more. I don't have the same kind of relationship with him as you do with Nivea."

"I ain't got shit wit her."

"Wasn't that her you were talking to just a few minutes ago?"

"And where the fuck she at?"

Jazmin shrugged.

"Exactly," he responded. He asked, "So why the fuck that nigga here?"

"I extended the offer to be nice."

Jah walked over to the side of the bed she was on. Looking down at her he asked, "So why you been crying? Do I need to fuck somebody up? Did that pretty doctor mufucka do somethin' to you? I'll fuck him up."

She shook her head feeling as though she was lying. The truth was Lamar needed to be fucked up for what he done. "I'm alright. You can go back upstairs."

"What if I don't wanna go?"

Jazmin cut her eyes at him and sucked her teeth. "Don't even try it Jah."

"Try what?" his voice held humor in it. He reached out for her but she pushed him away.

"Go on!" she said firmly.

"I can't touch you now?"

"Go touch Nivea."

"I wanna touch Juicy," he said playfully while grabbing at her.

Jazmin moved over on the bed. "So I'm Juicy again huh?"

"You always Juicy," he told her. He crawled in the bed with her. She couldn't move over any further or she would be on the floor. Hovering over her, he studied her face. He asked, "Why was yo ass crying?"

"I told you; I don't feel good."

"I think yo ass lying."

She tried to push him away but he didn't budge. Instead he pressed into her. Jazmin tried to ignore the desire she had for him. She was just getting to a point where she was learning to accept that he didn't want her like that anymore. She didn't want to fall for Jah's shit to only be rejected later. *Hmmm,* she pondered. *Kinda like how I did him.*

Jah grinded into her center and asked, "You feel that?"

Jazmin nodded. She definitely felt him growing hard against her. She looked up into his eyes. Eyes that always expressed how Jah truthfully felt whether he was mad or sad, even when he didn't want people to know. The same eyes that she adored that held so much love whenever he looked at Genesis. That same love was always present when he looked at her too. Why had it taken her so long to figure all of this out?

She asked softly, "Have I lost you?"

"Naw," he answered without much thought.

She reached up and caressed her fingers across his brow. She smiled because Genesis' brows were exactly like his. The older Genesis got, the more evident who her father was. The tests had proven without a doubt that Jah had been the one to impregnate her. She never told Jah the results because he had made it clear he didn't want to do the test and didn't care about the results.

She said, "I love you. It took me a minute to admit it to myself but I do; I love you."

"Now you wanna get all mushy and shit," he joked.

"I owe you a lot of 'I love you's' Jah."

Instead of responding to her verbally, Jah leaned in and placed a kiss on her lips. Jazmin didn't want their lip encounter to be over with so she kissed him back forcing his lips to part.

They were locked in a deep sensual kiss for what seemed like forever. When Jah finally forced himself away, he told her, "You know you done started somethin'."

Jazmin nodded as her heart raced wildly.

His hand slithered up under her dress rubbing in between her thick thighs where the warmth of her sweetness radiated. Without a fight, she willingly opened up for him. He pushed up sitting back on his haunches to tug her panties down. But removing her panties wasn't enough. The whole dress needed to go. She assisted him in removing it until she laid before him naked.

His eyes roamed her entire body. She didn't feel self-conscious as she had months before. She was ready to accept that when Jah said he loved all of her, then that was the honest truth. She had to believe that he truly cherished her body. And the way he was caressing her body with his hands in that moment only reassured her of how much he adored her.

His hand rubbed her stomach as he said, "I'm sorry I wasn't there for you when you lost the baby."

She looked away from his gaze. At the time she was going through the miscarriage she was upset with him, but she didn't want to dwell on that.

"We can make anotha one though," he said.

She returned her gaze to him as she watched him removing his shirt. She had seen his body enough times to know when a new tattoo was present. She stared at Genesis' name along his collar bone. She reached out and traced it with her finger. She asked, "When did you do this?"

"A few weeks ago," he answered.

She teased, "Where's my name?"

"I ain't puttin' no woman's name on me," he replied.

Jazmin eyed his mother's and sister's name tatted on his neck.

He quickly said, "They don't count."

Jazmin reached out and tugged at his jeans. "Just get these off."

Impatiently she watched him undress. It seemed as though he was moving deliberately slow to torment her. Once he moved himself back in between her legs, she locked him in by wrapping her legs around him. They kissed aggressively. His chest grazing her nipples intensified the ache in them. She moved her hips forward when she felt his hand in search of her wetness.

Their kiss finally broke when she pulled away enjoying the sensation of his dick head rubbing the wetness of her up and down her slit. She winced and bit down on her bottom lip when she felt him enter her. His stroke game had her gone. His steady deep and even paced strokes already had her trembling. She tried to stifle her moans but a few escaped her lips.

"I miss yo' ass," Jah whispered to her.

Jazmin thrust back on him as he kissed her here and there on her neck until he was able to tend to her breasts. Her nipples were hurting like hell but the pleasure was much more enjoyed than the discomfort.

He said, "You feel so good to me Juicy."

She answered him with moans.

He picked up the pace and he went harder. It wasn't enough. He needed her on all fours. It was something about pounding her from behind that drove him crazy.

Once she got in position, he pressed her back with his hand gesturing that he needed her to lower her body to the bed and have her ass in the air as much as possible. After working himself in her, he grabbed her by the hips as he picked up the pace. She tried to hang in there with him but it was too much. She took the dip out of her back and inched closer to the edge of the bed.

"Where the fuck you think you goin?" Jah asked. "Yo ass finna be on the goddamn floor."

"It's too much," she panted.

"Naw, it's never too much. Take this shit. You a big girl. You can take this dick Juicy," he told her. He started pounding in her with an unrelenting passion. She wanted to scream.

He finally pushed her over on her side and positioned himself in between her legs with one over his shoulder. He started pumping in and out of her slowly. Her moans came out as soft whimpers. He bent down to kiss her. "You like that shit huh?"

"Yes," she groaned.

"You sure you love me?"

A smile eased on her lips as she shook her head to mess with him.

"Don't make me act up in this pussy," he threatened.

She flashed him a sneaky smile as she closed her eyes. That's all he needed to see before he commenced to putting a pounding on her pussy.

"Fuck!" she hollered. She started punching him. He just grinned at her wickedly.

"I hate you—Oh shit!" she screamed.

"Shut the fuck up!" he hissed. He continued to dig even harder and deeper.

Jazmin couldn't take much more. She shoved at his hips and pushed back at the same time. "Stop Jah!"

"You want me to really stop?"

"No but—"

"That's what I thought."

———

The fireworks sounded off back to back. They should have been on the upper decks with everyone else enjoying the show however they decided to watch from their cabin's window. It wasn't as a beautiful scene but at least they didn't miss them entirely.

Jah held Jazmin from behind taking in the scent of her hair, cherishing the feel of her naked body against his, and loving their intimacy.

He broke the quietness as he spoke carefully. "I fucked up Juicy. I wasn't thinking when I did that shit to Sean."

"I know you weren't," she replied softly. "But it happened."

"Yeah, but now I gotta be without you and Genni."

Not getting what he was saying, she asked, "Why do you say that?"

He took in a breath and let it out before answering. "I'm going back to prison."

She gasped in disbelief. Turning around to face him, she asked, "How do you know? Don't Lu got you a good lawyer?"

"Yeah he do, but the prosecutor on the case ain't fuckin' budging. She's determined to make my ass do time. And 'less they work out a deal, she gon take this shit to trial. If it go to trial, I could be facing a harsher sentence. Even with Sean not saying nothin' the state can still move forward with trying my ass. Bitch ass prosecution seem to think they got enough fuckin' evidence without Sean's testimony that a jury will find my ass guilty."

"How much time?"

"Enough that I want you to forget about my ass."

"That's not gonna happen."

"Don't stress about that shit. I don't even want you to care."

Jazmin angered a little. "How fair is that Jah?"

"It ain't no fuckin different then all them other times in the past when my ass got locked up."

"It is different!" she snapped. "We got a child together now!"

Jah turned away from her to lay on his back. "What the fuck can I be for yall if I'm locked up? Not a goddamn thing."

"But it's still not fair for you to expect me not to care just because you don't."

"The fuck you mean? I do care but caring 'bout the shit ain't gon change the fuckin' outcome. That's why I ain't been fuckin wit you lately."

Tears burned her eyelids. She said, "That's why? You made it seem as if I had done something to you. You treated me like crap Jah. I tried to be there for you and you basically shut the door on me. And it's not fair, because you would rather spend all your days with Nivea instead of trying to make memories with me before you go."

"That ain't what the fuck I'm sayin!" he gritted.

Heated, she asked, "Then what the fuck are you saying?"

"It's gon hurt!" he shouted. "I don't wanna feel that shit when it's time for me to go! That shit ain't mothafuckin' easy for me Jazmin. I'm already fucked up knowing I gotta leave my babygirl behind. I'd just rather you move the fuck on now. Don't even fuckin worry 'bout me. But hell, ain't this why you ain't never wanted to fuck with me in the first goddamn place? All my stupid ass ever do is find some mothafuckin' way back to prison."

"I'm disappointed but I'm not trying to dismiss you out of me and Genni's life like that. You can't expect me to."

Somberly he said, "I'ma a fuckin disappointment. I see me failing to be what I fuckin' need to be fo' Genni and fo' you. I just wanted you to move on from me."

"But me and you is something you've been wanting. Now that we're at that place, you wanna push me away."

"Yeah, that was befo' this shit. Just do what you always do...'Fuck Jah'."

Jazmin looked on defeated as he sat up on the other side of the bed. When she saw he was reaching for his clothes, she asked, "Where are you going?"

"Back up there."

Irritated she said, "You're always leaving."

"It's what I do best!" he retorted.

"No," she called commanding his attention. He looked back at her. "No what?"

"No. Don't leave this time. Stay down here with me," she said in a pleading tone. She reached out for him.

What was it going to hurt? Besides, pretty soon he wouldn't be in Jazmin's presence. He needed to take advantage of the time he could get with her and Genesis.

Jah decided to get comfortable again beside Jazmin's body. He put his arms around her and she snuggled closer into his chest.

Jazmin said, "Let's make this work Jah. Forget those other two people we invited."

"What does that mean Juicy? Didn't you hear me say I was going back to prison?"

"Let's not claim that. I have faith that Lu and his lawyers will get you through this."

"So what the fuck does making this work mean?"

Jazmin looked over her shoulder at him. "It means, no more arguing and fighting. It means, you come back to me and Genni."

"To the house?"

"Yeah. Isn't your condo occupied?"

"Them mothafuckas still can't stay there like that," Jah rebutted.

Jazmin let out a soft laugh. "Jah! Don't be so mean. If your daddy and his...his...what is she to him? Don't you know this whole time I thought she was there for you?"

"I know you did. I wasn't gonna correct yo assuming ass either. You always take some shit and run with it."

"I do," she said in agreement. "I'm gonna do better."

"We'll see," Jah mumbled. His hand began to rub her stomach affectionately. "If I knew for sho' that I wasn't goin' back to prison, I'd wanna try for another baby now."

"Like what we just did was protected?" Jazmin joked.

"That didn't make no baby."

Jazmin laughed. "How do you know?"

"I know," he said playfully. "I knew when I put Genni's lil fat ass up in yo guts."

Jazmin giggled. "No you didn't. Shut up Jah."

Chapter 9

The following mid-morning, a very physically exhausted and drained but emotionally rejuvenated Jazmin walked off the boat smiling a little too hard. Her bright and fresh face was annoying to Tanya who wasn't in the best of moods.

"I thought yall got off last night," Jazmin was saying to Tanya as they approached her car.

"She ain't told you, huh?" Cassie interjected.

"Told me what?" Jazmin asked looking upside Tanya's head.

Pouting and wearing a frown, Tanya said, "That nigga went home with Nivea."

"Who?" cluelessly asked Jazmin.

Cassie found amusement in filling Jazmin in. "Oh yeah, while you were down at the bottom of the boat getting boinked by your baby daddy, Tyrell turns out to be Nivea's husband."

Jazmin halted in her stride with her mouth hung open in disbelief. "Shut up!"

Tanya rolled her eyes upward and released an irritated breath. "Yeah, ain't this world fucked up and small than a mothafucka."

Jazmin quickened her pace to catch up with Tanya and Cassie. She said jokingly, "By the way, I wasn't getting 'boinked' by my baby daddy."

Cassie laughed. "Oh yes you were! I came looking for you and it didn't take me long to figure out which room yall was in. You freaky mothafuckas! I mean, what is it with yall? Every time a large group of people congregate, that's when yall wanna decide to fuck."

Jazmin covered her mouth to stifle her giggles. "Did you hear us for real?"

"Yes!" Cassie shrieked. She started mocking Jazmin, "*Oh Jah! Yes! Stop it Jah! You play too much! Yeah...right there! Fuck!*"

Jazmin laughed and hit Cassie's arm playfully.

Cassie added, "Besides, after Jah put you to sleep the first time, he came back up confirming what I heard was correct."

Jazmin gasped covering her mouth. "He left out of the room?"

"The nigga was thirsty," Cassie laughed.

"And he told?"

"Well, he didn't exactly tell," Cassie explained. "We were teasing him and he was blushing kinda hard. I didn't think his mean ass could blush like that. But him love him some Juicy baby!"

Jazmin hit Cassie again playfully in the arm. "Stop it!"

A disgruntled Tanya cut her eyes towards them, "Will yall stop playing and c'mon. I just wanna get home."

The three ladies reached Jazmin's jeep. Before getting in the passenger's side, Cassie said to her close friend, "Tanya, fuck that nigga. It was something about him I ain't liking anyway. You can do better than his ass."

"But he's Tyriq's daddy," Tanya reasoned sadly.

"So!" Cassie countered. "That doesn't mean you gotta take his shit either. Put that jailbird ass nigga on child support and make sure you ask the judge for back pay too. Shit, my Spidey senses is telling me that nigga like to put his hands on women. You saw how he snatched Nivea up last night and basically dragged that bitch off the boat last night."

"Really?" Jazmin asked in disbelief. She looked over at Tanya sympathetically. "Yeah, Tanya you don't need a man like that."

Tanya frowned shaking her head. She said, "I guess I'll see yall later. Jazmin, call me some time tomorrow."

Cassie and Jazmin bid Tanya farewell. Once in her driver's seat and after immediately rolling the windows down, Jazmin asked, "So did you and Rock make up?"

Cassie looked ahead through the front windshield. Her eyes followed Rock as he stood amongst a group of men talking. He seemed perfectly fine as if her silent treatment had little to no effect on him. She turned up her nose in disdain, "Fuck Rodney Jamison."

Jazmin chuckled as she ignited her vehicle to life. "You called him by his government. You still mad at him?"

Cassie pointed towards where Rock stood. "Do he look like he care about my ass?"

"You know how men are," Jazmin said matter of factly. She reached out to adjust her air conditioning settings. "They got big egos and hate to admit to anything, especially when they're wrong."

"Tuh," Cassie scoffed. "He admitted he fucked Michelle."

"Wait! What?"

"He went ahead and admitted it after denying it for a week. So fuck Rodney Jamison!"

"Damn," Jazmin said under her breath in thought. She looked over at Cassie and asked cautiously, "You didn't get the...you know...the cabin confession cooties?"

Cassie couldn't help but to laugh. "Shut up Jazz! No, I didn't."

"I'm just saying," Jazmin said widening her eyes for emphasis.

A rapid knocking on Jazmin's driver's side door startled both women. When Jazmin saw who it was standing outside her door, she instantly soured.

"What?" she asked flatly.

"Can we speak for a second?" Lamar asked.

"I thought you left last night," Jazmin said.

"No, I actually passed out on the upper deck," he told her. He stepped aside indicating he wanted her out of the car.

"Can we talk later," Jazmin bargained. "I gotta take Cass home and it's hot."

"It won't take but a minute," Lamar insisted.

Cassie sang discreetly under her breath, "That nigga's worrisome."

"We'll talk," Jazmin said trying to brush him off. She prepared to put her car in drive.

Desperately, Lamar asked, "What did I do to you Jazmin?"

"I said, we'll talk later," Jazmin repeated firmly.

"Are you getting back with Jah?" he asked.

Cassie threw her hands up in exasperation. "Dude! She said she'll talk to you later. If you had any sense you'd back away from the car now and hop your big ass in your lil car."

"I wasn't talking to you—" Lamar was saying but was interrupted as he was shoved aside.

"Getcho' bald headed ass out the way mufucka," Jah snarled while mean mugging Lamar.

Cassie mumbled, "I told his ass."

Jazmin reprimanded, "Jah! Please don't—"

"Shut up," Jah snapped playfully. He leaned inside the window to give Jazmin a nice wet kiss.

"Ugh!" Jazmin laughed. "Will you stop?"

Jah turned his attention back to Lamar, "Why you still standin' here nigga?"

"I was talking to—"

"Bye mufucka!" Jah barked.

"Jah," Jazmin warned calmly.

"I'll just talk to you later Jazmin," Lamar was saying as he turned to walk away.

"No yo' ass won't either," Jah told him. "As a matter of fact, stay yo ass away from Juicy. Aint' shit yall gotta talk about no mo'. She off limits to yo mufuckin' ass. And lemme catch yo gay ass around her, I'ma—"

"Jah!" Jazmin called out to him. "Stop and leave him alone."

"I want that bald headed mufucka to know yo ass is all me," Jah spoke as he glared at Lamar's back as he walked away. "Sissy ass nigga. He even walk gay. Watch how his ass gotta fold up to get in that lil ass car. Big ass nigga. Fuck him."

Cassie was in the passenger's seat dying with laughter.

Jah turned to Jazmin. In a serious tone he asked, "What we talked about is how things gon be, right?"

Jazmin nodded.

"Then I don't wanna see his big bald headed ass around for nothin' no mo'," Jah told her.

"Yeah, I know Jah," Jazmin said.

Cassie still struggled through her fit of giggles.

Jazmin threw out to him, "That goes for you too."

"You ain't gotta worry 'bout me. My shit handled," Jah said.

Jazmin gave him a doubting look. "Oh really?"

"Trust me," he told her. He leaned in the window once more to peck her on the lips. "I'll be at the house later. Give me a minute."

Jazmin nodded. She watched him walk away as he stopped briefly to speak to the group of guys. He then headed to his car. Jazmin sighed dreamily.

Cassie teased, "Aw! Yall finally getting it together."

"Yeah," Jazmin smiled. "I'm gonna stop fighting it and just let things be."

"That's good," Cassie said with thought. She asked, "Are you getting married?"

Jazmin shook her head as she snorted a laugh. "No one is talking marriage."

"Yall should," Cassie threw out there.

"Jah, is not the marrying type," Jazmin said. She proceeded to drive down the graveled driveway tapping her horn and waving to a few people as she passed.

"You don't know that," Cassie said. She teased with a grin, "You can make a hood nigga into a husband."

"The word marriage don't even sound right coming out of Jah's mouth," Jazmin pointed out.

"Well, yall wasn't married with Genni. But if yall gonna keep on having babies, yall might as well do it all the way right."

"Who said anything about having babies?"

Cassie didn't respond.

Jazmin took her eyes off of the road for a second to look at Cassie with question. Cassie was wearing a knowing smirk.

"What do you...What's all that for?" Jazmin asked trying to hold back her giggles.

Cassie hummed a little tune as she looked out of her window. She said, "I be knowing Jazz."

———

Georgia couldn't quite put her finger on it, but she knew something was going on with Jah. Whatever it was, she needed it to continue to happen. He was in better spirits on this day more than he had been any other day since Sheena died.

"What's gotten into you?" Georgia asked. She stood at the threshold of her kitchen area with her usual prop in hand: a dish towel.

"Who me?" Jah asked. He tossed Kelan on the sofa and pushed Kaleb by the head. The boys tried to retaliate but Jah kept pushing them away.

182

"Yes you. Will yall stop and leave your big cousin alone?" Georgia said to her grandsons. "Take yall asses downstairs and mess with your granddaddy."

"When our mama coming?" Kaleb asked as they trudged to the staircase.

"Don't worry 'bout that," Georgia censured. "She get here when she get here."

Kelan said cheerfully, "I wanna stay here anyway."

Jah couldn't help but to mock Kelan as he always did. He chuckled, "Lil white ass."

Georgia turned her attention back to Jah. "So how was the boat ride? I heard they do it up. It's better than riding the General Jackson."

"That country shit!" Jah said as if he was offended. He sat on the couch, but in a way so that he could still face his aunt.

"You swear Jah like yo' ass ain't country," Georgia chuckled.

"But the General Jackson? C'mon Auntie. Ain't no mufuckin comparison."

"I'm just saying," she shrugged. "So how was it?"

"That shit was nice," he told her.

"You stayed on it overnight?"

He nodded. "By the time it made it back out to Abe's house out there in the country, hell, it didn't make no fuckin' sense to get off."

"I bet Nivea enjoyed that, huh?"

"Fuck Nivea," Jah said dismissively.

Georgia rolled her eyes upward. "Oh Lord! What she done did now?"

"Her husband out," he told Georgia.

"Is he?" Georgia asked in shock.

Jah was about to respond until he felt something brush against his leg. Without giving it much thought, he reacted and accidentally kicked Mittenz. She yelped which made Jah laugh.

"Sorry, I didn't see yo lil ass down there," he said. He reached out for the dog and placed her in his lap. Sox was closely behind. Without an invitation she leaped up on the couch and tried to steal Jah's attention.

"They really like their uncle Jah," Georgia teased.

Since Sheena's passing, her dogs provided Jah a comfort and a sense of Sheena's presence. He knew how much they meant to her, so it was only right for him to care for them as Sheena would.

"We gon be leaving," Jah told Georgia as he rubbed through Mittenz fur.

"Going where? You taking the dogs?"

"Yep. Me and my nieces goin' home," he beamed.

"Home? Your daddy and Gina done moved out the condo?"

Jah shook his head. "Naw. I'm talkin' 'bout we finna be at Juicy's."

"Wait a minute," Georgia said with her hand on her hip. "You left yesterday with Nivea to get on the boat. You got off the boat and came back talking about moving in with your baby mama. What's going on Jah?"

He shrugged with a coy smile. "Me and my baby made up."

Georgia grinned. "It's about damn time! Yall need to be together. Don't make no sense the way yall go back and forward like that and being with people you really don't like."

"Yeah we said that," he told her in agreement.

"Yall talked about this?"

Jah nodded.

Frowning with confusion, Georgia asked, "Well let me ask you this. If Nivea's husband is back, why she go with you yesterday?"

"Long fuckin' story," Jah said getting up. Sox and Mittenz were prepared to follow him.

"That nigga was on the boat. And guess who the fuck he was with?"

"Who?"

"Tanya, Juicy's lil fat friend. That nigga the daddy to her lil crusty nose ass son."

Georgia giggled. "Stop that Jah. Don't be talking about her son."

"He look like his bowling ball head ass daddy too," Jah mentioned. He started walking towards the hallway. He called over his shoulder, "Ay, I'm finna get my shit real quick."

Georgia stood there shaking her head as she watched the two dogs trailing behind their new master. She turned to tend to her duties in the kitchen but a knock came from her front door.

"Who the hell is this?" she muttered under her breath. She made her way to the picture window in her living room to peek out at her porch. Amusingly, she opened her door and cracked her storm door just enough. "Hey."

Nivea smiled, "Hey."

Georgia glanced towards Nivea's house and didn't see any signs of a man. She looked back at Nivea, "I heard your old man back."

"Jah told you, huh?"

"Yep. Where he at cause I don't want you bringing no mess to my nephew. Jah already dealing with enough. If he kick your husband's ass, that's another charge for him."

Nivea grinned awkwardly thinking that Georgia was joking, but the stern look on Georgia's face told her otherwise. "He's not here."

"Well don't you think you need to get on back to your house before he come back?"

"No, he's not living with me," Nivea explained. "I saw Jah's car here and I wanted to talk to him."

Georgia ignored Nivea's last comment. She asked, "He ain't living with you? Where he at then?"

Nivea shrugged. "I guess with his baby mama."

"Wait, ain't you his wife and he got kids with you?"

"He's not my kids' real daddy," she explained.

"He ain't?" Georgia was shocked.

Nivea tried again, "Can I speak to Jah."

Ignoring her again, Georgia said, "All this time I thought he was your kids' daddy. Yall ain't got no kids together?"

Nivea shook her head. She heard Jah's voice when he asked, "Who you talkin' to Auntie?"

Georgia stood in the opening of the door and said over her shoulder, "It ain't nobody. Go on and do whatchu was doing."

Appalled, Nivea said, "So I'm a nobody Ms. Georgia?"

Hearing her voice, Jah opened the door wider. "What the fuck you want?"

"I wanted to talk to you," Nivea said. She shifted her eyes to Georgia. "That's all."

"We ain't got shit to talk 'bout," Jah said.

"Tee is gone," Nivea told him in hopes he would listen. "We're not together anymore."

Georgia looked at Jah, "You got this? I need to get back to my ribs. Your Uncle Milton threw down on that grill yesterday. Meat just fall right off the bone!"

As Georgia hurried away, Jah called out to her, "Save me some Auntie!"

Nivea blew air in frustration to get his attention.

Jah turned to her and decided to step fully onto the porch closing the door behind him. "Why you over here man?"

"To talk to you. I made Tee leave," she explained.

"So."

"So? I made him leave so that you and I could continue what we had going."

"You tell him we been fuckin?"

"No; he don't need to know all that."

"I ain't fuckin witchu Niv. I'd have to kill that nigga cause he ain't the type that know how to be mufuckin quiet and keep to his damn self. He gotta be seen and mufuckin heard, ol' pussy ass nigga."

"He's going to your friend's house to be with her. He won't bother us."

"You damn right he won't bother us cause it ain't no mothafuckin us!"

"Oh really? So it's you and Jazmin again? How long is that going to last before you come knocking on my door?"

"Hol' up! First off, I ain't never had to knock on yo' goddamn do' cause yo ass was over here all up in my face. Hell, you didn't even give me a mothafuckin chance to chase yo ass. Soon as I showed interest, you was showing up at my auntie's house for dumb ass shit just to be seen. Don't come at me with that stupid ass bullshit!"

"Fuck you Jah!" Nivea spat. "You didn't turn me down. And you were all into me when Jazmin didn't give a fuck about you. You were the one that kept asking about when my husband was getting out."

"Damn right! I wanted to mufuckin know so I could stop fuckin' wit yo ass cause I ain't want no shit."

"So you were using me?"

"If that's what you wanna call it," he said flippantly.

"You so fucking confused," she said with disgust.

Jah gave her statement some thought. He responded, "Naw. I was just stupid for a second after my sister died. I ain't fuckin' confused. Juicy is who I want, always wanted, and always will want."

"That's who you were with last night?"

"You mothafuckin' guessed it!"

Nivea rolled her eyes in an exaggerated manner. "I knew you were with her."

"Well if you knew it, why the fuck you over here?"

"Because," she answered. She looked at him desperately. "I got feelings for you that I can't just turn off Jah."

"What the fuck I'm 'posed to do? Show you where the mufuckin' switch at?"

"I hate you!" she yelled.

"There it go," Jah laughed. He went for the door. "Man, I got shit to do and somewhere to mufuckin be. I'll holla atchu later."

Nivea went for Jah's arm to stop him. "Wait Jah."

Jah looked back at her hand on his arm. "Getcho hands off me."

"Stop being like that," she told him. "You know this thing with you and Jazmin won't work. You know that. You've said it before yourself."

Before Jah could answer, a silver Chevrolet Cruze slowed down in front of his aunt's house only to pull up in Nivea's driveway. Nivea turned to see what Jah was looking at and saw Tyrell exiting the car. Tyrell glared over in their direction and Nivea instantly released Jah.

Jah scoffed shaking his head, "You full of shit, ol' shaky ass. Get off my auntie's porch and go over there to yo' nigga."

Chapter 10

For the hundredth time, Jazmin hit ignore on her phone. Lamar was calling her back to back. She would have thought he had gotten it after the first five times he called and she sent him to voicemail. She didn't even understand what he could possibly want.

"Oh my God!" she groaned with frustration.

"Just answer the phone for him one time," Desiree said on the other end of the phone.

"No. I have nothing to talk to him about at the moment," Jazmin said. She looked over at Genesis relaxing comfortably in her cradling swing. She was wide awake but Jazmin could tell Genesis was debating on reaching for the plush elephant toys dangling above her.

"What did Lamar do now?"

"I just don't wanna talk about him," Jazmin said busying herself tidying an already spotless kitchen.

"Okay," Desiree breathed. "So how was the boat ride?"

"It was good," she answered as she thought of her conversation with Landrus. "I was a lil sick for half of the day."

"That must have sucked."

Jazmin smiled, "Not too much. Jah ended up in the cabin where I was lying down."

"Oh really?" Desiree was piqued. "So what did you two do in the room?"

"We did a lot of talking."

"And?"

"And that was it," Jazmin answered with a chuckle.

"Did yall do it?"

"Well...of course we got around to that."

"You two! Didn't he invite Nivea and didn't you invite Lamar? Another repeat of the mountains, huh?"

"I guess," Jazmin shrugged. "Things just end up that way."

"Yeah...whatever. When are you two going to stop this thing you two do with each other?"

"I told you we talked. He and I decided to give us a fair try. We're putting all of the dumb shit—as Jah calls it—aside."

"About time!" Desiree exclaimed.

"Oh shut up Dez," Jazmin dismissed. "What about you and Damien?"

"I'm not talking to him," Desiree answered dryly.

"Why? Did you tell him you were pregnant?"

"Nope. I was almost tempted to tell him the last time he called."

"Wait. He's been calling you?"

"Yeah and I decided to answer the last call he made today. He tried to convince me that there was nothing going on with him and Rayven. He said he went by to talk to Sean. He tried to say that when he text Sean earlier that day, he told him he was at home but of course Sean wasn't there. So Rayven convinced him to stay and keep him company."

"Do you believe him?"

"Jazz, if I believed him, he'd probably be here at home with me," Desiree chuckled.

"You're right," Jazmin said. A nostalgic sound put an instant smile on her face. "Hey, let me call you back."

"Okay," Desiree said. She teased, "Is that your boo or something?"

"Bye Dez," Jazmin sang into the phone before ending the call.

Jazmin headed to the front door. She stepped out onto the porch. She asked Jah as he got out of his car, "Why didn't you pull in the garage?"

"Cause I gotta leave back out to take this lil nigga home," he answered. He went to the backseat and pulled out a giggling little boy. "C'mon lil punk."

"You punk!" Caiden laughed.

Jazmin smiled realizing how good it felt to know that the little boy Jah was holding was his baby brother.

"You brought company," Jazmin cheered.

"Wait, there's more," Jah said while putting Caiden down next to her.

Jazmin looked down at Caiden. "Hi. I'm Jazmin."

"This you…you…house?"

"It sure is. You wanna come inside?"

"I jus wanna watch stach man."

"Huh?" Jazmin asked as she opened the door for Caiden to step inside.

"Stach man. You not got stach man?" Caiden asked. He proceeded to walk down the hallway as if he knew the layout of Jazmin's house.

"What are you saying?" Jazmin asked as she followed Caiden to the den.

Genesis babbling and squealing caught Caiden's attention. He walked over to her and she got quiet as she focused on him.

"This my sister."

Jazmin chuckled, "No. Actually she's your niece."

"What's a niece?"

Little tapping noises distracted Jazmin. Mittenz and Sox were running around in her kitchen sniffing everything. She looked at Jah who was wearing a goofy grin. "Uhm...why do I have two white furballs in my kitchen?"

"I couldn't leave 'em Juicy," Jah explained. He walked up to her and kissed her forehead. "They my lil nieces."

"What's a nieces?" Caiden asked. He walked towards the den area. "Why her house big? It get bigger and bigger and bigger."

"Go sitcho bigger and bigger ass down," Jah told Caiden.

"Jah!" Jazmin scolded. "Don't talk to him like that."

"That lil nigga talk to me any kinda way; so I'ma dish that shit back out to him."

"Shut up big head!" Caiden yelled.

"See what the fuck I'm talkin' 'bout?" Jah said to Jazmin. "Nigga ain't got no goddamn home training."

Jazmin teased, "Well you're big brother so you can teach him."

"Shit," Jah murmured as he walked over to the sink.

Jazmin watched him splatter water everywhere as he washed his hands. She also watched him not bothering to wipe up the puddles of water he created around the sink. Typical Jah. She immediately went behind him after he walked over to pick Genesis up.

"Hey—" Jah began but was interrupted with a laugh from Genesis.

Jazmin stopped wiping and gasped. "Did she just laugh?"

"I think—"

Genesis started cracking up. She paused waiting for Jah to speak again.

Jazmin grew excited. "My baby is laughing now! That's right, laugh at your silly daddy."

"Stop laughing at me lil thickumz," Jah said to Genesis which sent her into another fit of laughter. He looked at Jazmin and said, "Yo baby is officially retarded too."

———

Cassie knew by agreeing to let Rock come by she was setting herself up. She had remained single for so long just to avoid these types of situations. She told herself she didn't want to be one of those women like she witnessed her friends being, gullible and naïve. She wasn't built to tolerate a lot of bullshit from a man. Although she was hurt by his actions, Cassie had to admit that she honestly missed Rock's company. He had grown on her during the times they hung together.

"You ain't gotta look so angry," Rock said to her.

She released a breath of frustration. "Why did you wanna come by here Rodney?"

He smiled displaying the slightly chipped tooth that she had always been fond of, even in their youth.

Remaining cold and stone-faced, she said, "Why are you smiling? There's nothing to be smiling about?"

"Why I can't smile Cass?"

"Cause you ain't over here to be serious," she said. She got up to head to her front door.

Rock caught her by her hand and pulled her right back down next to him. "Stop tripping. Stop being so damn mean and loosen your ass up."

Cassie snatched her hand back. "Why you fuck Michelle?"

Rock opened his mouth to answer but was interrupted by Cassie. She threw out another question. "Why ain't you getting your hair cut?"

With his mouth still open he tried to answer.

"When you getting a car?"

He just stared at her at this point.

"When the last time you seen your kids?"

"Man, what the fuck is this?" Rock finally asked with vexation.

"Since you here, I might as well ask everything. So back to the number one question: Why you fuck Michelle?"

Before he spoke he licked his lips in a way that Cassie wished she hadn't witnessed. Was this what it felt like to be weak? Her woman parts were aroused. The thing about Rock was that even though he was the most broke of all of their friends, he was the cutest. He was thirty-two but had a boyish baby face that gave him the innocence of a freshly graduated high school boy. Certain things that he did in his mannerisms, such as licking his lips, gave that baby face an undeniable sexiness. It took Cassie a while before she could see past everything else to really appreciate Rock. But being that he slept with Michelle she was beginning to think she should have just left things the way they were.

"I fucked her 'cause it was something to do; that's all. It was before you let me hit. Way before."

"If it was way before, then why she tried to say the baby she carrying could be yours?"

"I don't know. To fuck with you I guess. I didn't know the hoe was pregnant but I covered up anyway. I used my own poppa stoppas too. I don't want no mo' kids."

That was disappointing to hear. Maybe ending their little fling and going back to being just friends was best.

"How many times?" Cassie asked.

"How many times what?"

"Did you fuck her. How many fuckin times!" Cassie asked angrily.

"There you go with that angry shit," Rock said cutting his eyes at her. "Calm the fuck down."

"You can go then," she said trying to get up.

"Stop man," Rock said preventing her from getting up. "What's knowing that gonna do?"

"Cause if it was nothing between yall, I'm wondering what could have made you hit her back up for seconds and thirds."

"There was no seconds or thirds. Only that one time. I did take her on a few rounds though," he said with humor laced in his voice.

"See that's the shit I'm talking about," Cassie hissed angrily. She moved his arm away from her and she stood up. "Get out! Take your broke ass and go on Rock. We cool just being friends."

Rock looked up at her wearing a grin. "You don't want me to go nowhere."

"Oh yes the fuck I do!" she exclaimed.

"Why your titties say different?"

"Fuck you!" she said angrily. She walked over to her door. "Let's go Rock. I'm 'bout to take my ass to sleep and you need to go."

"Can I go to sleep with you?" he teased.

"No!"

"Okay, I quit. I'm being serious now," he assured her. "Come on back over here lil mama."

"Nope," she said defiantly.

"C'mon Cassie baby. Let's talk for real."

"You too fuckin childish Rock. I don't even know why I gave in to your ass," she pouted.

"I'm only childish sometimes," he joked.

Cassie blew out a breath in frustration while shaking her head.

"And you know why you gave in to my ass. I mean, I knew you wanted me to have the pussy. You was just tryna make a nigga work for it. I get that. But I know your ass started developing feelings for me. Just like I was for you."

"Whatever Rock!" she sang as she rolled her eyes.

"C'mere."

Cassie groaned. "Can you just leave?"

"After you come back over here."

"No, 'cause all you gon' do is try to touch on me and shit," Cassie snarled. "Ain't nobody got time for that."

"Damn you difficult," he stated as he shook his head. He got up and walked over to where Cassie was standing.

She folded her arms over her chest and stared him down. When a playful smile formed on his lips, she knew she was in trouble. Trying to remain firm in her stance, she rolled her eyes. When she sensed he was decreasing the space between them, she backed up into the wall and turned her lip up at him in disgust.

"Don't even try it," she grumbled.

Ignoring her and noticing her lack of a fight, Rock moved closer entrapping her between him and the wall.

"Stop all this shit," he told her in a pacifying but tempting tone.

Cassie couldn't make the wall budge to escape the kiss Rock planted on her lips that she put little effort in trying to prevent. *Ugh!* She was so mad with herself. She was being Jazmin, Tanya, and Rayven. She was letting her body lead instead of thinking with her brain. She had a quick conversation with herself in her head weighing reason and logic. She was convinced that she could do as men do. It was just sex. What was the harm in just getting sex and going about her business?

She broke their kiss long enough to say, "We can fuck and that's it; but then you gotta leave."

Rock started laughing. "What?"

"You heard me nigga," she said. She pushed him back to escape his trap. She headed to her bedroom.

Rock just stood there staring at her. He called out, "So you just using me now?"

"Ain't that what yall do!" she yelled over her shoulder. "And you better come on before I change my mind!"

———

After ending the call with her sister, Desiree couldn't resist the urge to call Damien. He had

203

eagerly answered. After a few short exchange of words, Damien was on his way back to the house.

While she waited, she contemplated whether or not if she would tell him about the pregnancy. One thing was for sure, she needed to know the truth about him and Rayven.

Damien let himself in to find a patiently waiting Desiree. She sat on the sofa in their living room.

"You're looking good," he told her.

She didn't say anything.

Damien cleared his throat as he took a seat across from her in the chair. "I thought you called me over here so that we could talk."

"I did," she said quietly.

"Let's talk."

Desiree smirked with a small laugh. "It's funny how before you got caught over Ray's you didn't want to talk things out with me. Do you consider this even now Damien?"

"I didn't do anything," Damien said defensively. "And I'm not seeking some revenge type of thing."

She gave him a skeptical look. "So you want me to believe that what Jazmin saw was nothing?"

"What did she see? I was upstairs and I came downstairs. I was fully clothed. Nothing happened."

"So why did you react the way you did? Jazz said you got nervous and was looking mighty guilty."

"What does Jazz know?" he asked with irritation.

"She know what she saw."

Sarcastically he said, "Oh yeah...I guess she would know a thing or two about guilt."

Desiree nodded her head slowly in realization. "So you're admitting to guilt."

"No! What I'm saying...Look, I know what it looked like. I didn't want her to get the wrong idea and it came out that way. And it didn't help matters that Rayven didn't bother to clear it up. It was almost as if that's what she wanted Jazmin and Sean to believe."

"So why were you there?"

"I already told you. Rayven mislead me. And since I was there she asked that I keep her company. We started talking about everything that has happened between all of us."

"Okay so you couldn't talk to me but you were willing to sit at another's woman house and talk to her and comfort her?"

"I didn't comfort her."

"Sitting there and talking with her is comforting Damien!" Desiree bellowed. "It was a hell of a lot more comforting than you walking out on me. And because of what reason Damien? Something I did before us?"

"It wasn't that!" he argued angrily. Realizing the loudness of his voice, Damien began to speak in a calmer tone. "If what you did before us didn't involve a man that I socialize with on a regular basis and that same man wasn't involved with your inability to get pregnant for us, then I wouldn't be as mad Desi. You gotta understand that. Don't you think I should have at least been made aware of the abortions? We were trying to have a baby and it was just as frustrating for me as it was for you, but at least you knew the reason. I was left in the dark."

Desiree swallowed the lump in her throat. She couldn't argue against his point. In a remorseful manner, she said, "I'm sorry. I could have – I mean I should have told you."

"That was my only point. But because you're so stubborn and hard to get through sometimes, you didn't even want to admit that you were wrong and hurtful in this whole situation. That's why I left. I take a lot of shit from you

Desiree because I love you. I know you are who you are and some things you just can't help because you're oblivious, but that...that was something I didn't want to look over and push aside."

Desiree lowered her head. "I know and I shouldn't expect you to. But...I need to know that you're telling me the truth about Rayven."

"Jesus!" Damien threw his hands up in exasperation. He got up abruptly to leave.

"Wait!" she called out to him desperately. She got up to follow behind him to the door.

Damien turned to her and asked, "Do you not trust me anymore Desi?"

Desiree's mouth open as she struggled to find words.

"I wouldn't do that to you," he told her as he searched her eyes. He needed her to believe that. He needed to see in her eyes that she believed him.

"I don't know," she mumbled. She looked away from his stare.

"You're the one that brought trust issues into our marriage. Before this we were good," he pointed out. He asked, "And after this, don't you want to be good?"

She looked back at him and nodded.

"So do you want to fix this?"

"How?" she asked.

Damien smiled, "Not by yourself of course. We can move on from this but we can't let things like this happen to us again. From now on, no more secrets."

"Okay," she spoke meekly.

"Can I come home?"

"I never told you to leave," she said.

"Okay, I'm coming home."

Desiree smiled but it suddenly began to fade.

Worried, Damien asked, "What is it?"

She cleared her throat and averted her eyes from his gaze. She said quietly, "Since there's no more secrets, there is something I need to tell you."

Damien sighed preparing himself for more bad news.

Desiree's eyes shifted back to his and she said, "We're pregnant."

It took a second for her words to sink in. Damien's eyes widened with excitement. "Preg— We're pregnant? You're pregnant?"

Desiree's smile returned and she nodded. She shrieked when Damien wrapped his arms around her and lifted her off the floor planting an endearing kiss on her lips.

"Okay, okay," she laughed. "Put me down!"

Damien lowered her back to the floor and asked, "How far along are you? When did you find this out? We haven't even went back for treatments."

"I know," she grinned. "I'm only like eight weeks. I didn't want anyone to really know because I wanted to make sure it would be a viable pregnancy. But I'm scared and I don't want to do this alone."

"You're not alone," Damien said as he took her into his arms. He kissed the top of her head. "I'm here and we got this."

Desiree felt assured by her husband's words; but she was still troubled by the unknown. This pregnancy had to make it.

The sight of Jah entering her bedroom put a smile on Jazmin's face. Never taking her eyes off of him, she sat up. She asked, "Is he sleep?"

"Naw, but I ain't finna stay in that mufucka til he fall asleep. I told you we shoulda took his lil ass home," Jah told her wearing his usual scowl.

"It's late and he asked to stay," Jazmin said. "Don't do your little brother like that."

Jah climbed in on his side of the bed. He said, "Genni's ass is out."

"I knew she would be," Jazmin said. The thought of Genesis' earlier fits of laughter put a bright smile on her face. "I can't believe she started laughing like that."

"Yeah, she gon be goofy like her fuckin' mama," Jah mumbled.

"Anyway," she dismissed. She asked, "So what is a 'stach man'?"

"A what?"

"Caiden...he kept saying he wanted to watch 'stach man'. I couldn't for the life of me figure out what he was saying."

Jah started laughing. "That nigga can't talk worth shit. He was saying 'scratch man' for Wolverine ass. You know the mufucka with the blades out his knuckles."

Jazmin started laughing also. "Oh! Scratch man...Wolverine. Okay. Well next time, I'll know."

"Hang around his lil ass long enough you'll be able to understand him. Nigga make up his own damn words."

Jazmin looked at Jah lovingly wearing a quirky smile. She knew the longer she stared at him, the more it would get him riled.

"What the fuck you looking at?" he asked.

She giggled. "You."

"Take yo' goofy ass to sleep," he murmured. He grabbed the remote from the nightstand turning his attention to the television.

Jazmin was enjoying Jah's presence already. She realized how much she really missed him. If she could have things her way, their relationship would go on forever. Even though Jah agreed to try to make things work, she knew if he went to prison, he would push her away. He already told her so during their talk about their relationship when they were on the boat. However Jazmin wasn't going to let him.

"Let's get married Jah," Jazmin blurted out.

"Man, go head on with that," he mumbled never taking his attention from the television.

"I'm serious. Let's get married before you go…if you go."

Jah finally looked at her. "Why the fuck you playin?"

Unsure of her own suggestion, Jazmin smile uneasily. "I'm not playing."

Jah continued to stare at her.

She reached over and removed the remote from his hand and placed it back on the nightstand. In doing so she had to stretch her body across his. Instead of returning to her side of the bed she decided to mount Jah instead.

A playful smile formed on his lips. "Whatchu doin Juicy?"

She didn't know what she was doing; she just needed him to listen to her. His arms moved to reach behind her to grope her ass but she caught both his arms by the wrists. She pinned his arms down by his side. She then lowered her body to his to kiss him softly on the lips. He wanted to hold her lips hostage but she broke away to plant suckling kisses along his neck.

"What the fuck you doin!" he squirmed.

Jazmin giggled as she continued. His hands went for her ass again and she tried to stop him from touching her but she wasn't fast enough.

Jah asked, "Where the fuck yo panties at witcho Lil Caesar's five dollar hot and ready ass?"

She grinned at him sneakily. She raised up enough to push his shirt up so that she could show his chest some affectionate attention. She worked her way quickly down his abdomen until she got to the waistband of his shorts. With no hesitation, she pulled his waistband down enough to free his growing erection. Again, no uncertainties or indecisiveness hindered her from instantly making love to him with her mouth.

In a sense she was being manipulative but she also enjoyed being able to please him. And with all of the hissing, groaning, and of course cursing Jah was doing, she felt like her actions were persuasive.

"Juicy," he groaned. He wanted to grab her head and fuck the shit out of her mouth but he didn't want to be disrespectful. But Jazmin definitely had some superb oral skills.

"Fuck this shit," he hissed. He grabbed her head and couldn't help it. He thrust his hips forward simultaneously with pushing her head further down on him and began jabbing the back of her throat aggressively.

Surprisingly, Jazmin kept up with his forcefulness longer than he thought she would. When she tried to take back control, he wouldn't let her so it irritated her.

"Stop Jah!" she yelled. She raised up glaring at him.

"Sorry...can't help it. You and yo goddamn mouf!"

Jazmin rolled her eyes as she wiped her mouth.

"Oh shut up," he said playfully. He reached for her. "C'mon and sitcho ass on this dick and stop playin."

A smile returned to Jazmin's face as she climbed back on top of him, this time working his dick inside her. Once he was snug inside her, she lowered her body to his and they locked lips in a long sensual kiss while their bodies moved in synchronization.

It was something different about the way they handled each other's bodies this time. It was a sense of security, a knowing that they were finally together as they should be.

Their uninhibited wild yet sensual lovemaking went on with no stops. They went from one position to the next, partially clothed to absolute nakedness. They were so caught up in each other that they didn't realize they had an audience.

Jazmin's head was hanging off the side of the bed while Jah sampled her goodness for the third time. She happened to open her eyes and noticed the two white furballs sitting by her dresser silently watching. She found it funny but instead of laughter, she opened her mouth to let out a long crying wail as her walls convulsed uncontrollably and another piece of her soul transferred to Jah as an intense orgasm waved through her body.

Both Mittenz and Sox tilted their heads to the side as she tried to gain back her composure. Breathless, she was able to finally laugh.

214

"What the fuck?" Jah noticed the two dogs for the first time. "You makin all that goddamn noise brought 'em in here. They wanted to see what the fuck was goin on."

Spent, Jazmin managed to slide back onto the bed. "They're weird. Make them get out."

"They aight," he chuckled. He lay across the bed next to her. He rubbed her belly and asked, "You sure yo' ass ain't still pregnant?"

Jazmin's eyes widen. She was thrown by that. She asked, "Why would you ask that?"

"'Cause," was all he said. He pushed down right above her navel. He asked, "Why is it hard right there?"

Self-consciously, she brushed his hand away and reached for the sheet to cover up. Jah gave her a look of skepticism.

Before he could ask her any more questions, she decided to get back the original mission for the night. She asked, "Do you remember a few months ago you said you and Daddy were talking about us and marriage? Were you serious then or was all that just talk?"

"Back to this marriage shit, huh?"

"Yes," she said definitely.

"Why would you wanna marry my ass knowing I'm finna go back to prison."

"I don't think you are Jah."

"Juicy, let's not even talk 'bout this shit." He turned away from her.

She moved close to him until she was pressed into his back. She moved his dreads out of the way so that she could rest her head against him while wrapping her arm around him.

Softly she said, "I won't talk about it anymore but know that marriage is something I want. Unlike the stupid mistakes I made with Sean, I don't wanna go about things with us like that. If we're gonna be together, then let's be together Jah...the right way."

There was silence.

Changing the subject to something a little lighter, Jazmin said in an upbeat tone, "Okay, how about if Lu's lawyer get your charges dropped, you gotta cut your dreads."

Jah found that amusing. "I ain't cutting my hair."

"Well you seem so sure you're going back to prison. If you're that sure, you'll do this bet with me."

"Okay, and if I go to prison whatchu gotta do?"

"What do you want me to do?"

Jah brought her hand up to his mouth to kiss. He pulled her arms around him tighter and said, "Just love me."

Chapter 11

The following morning, Jazmin and Genesis accompanied Jah to the condo to drop Caiden off to his parents.

"When I...when I coming back?" Caiden asked.

"Never," Jah answered as he let them inside the condo. Although he walked in first, there was little time to prevent Caiden from seeing what was happening before them.

Disgusted, Jah yelled, "Yall mothafuckas!"

Dewalis and Gina, who had been in the kitchen actively engaging in sexual activities on the counter, both scrambled to cover up their half exposed bodies.

"In my goddamn kitchen though!" Jah barked angrily.

Carrying Genesis, Jazmin walked in last after Mittenz and Sox wondering what was going on. She stepped around just in time to see Dewalis pulling up his pants and Gina ducking behind the kitchen's center island.

"Sorry...we didn't know...yall was—" Dewalis was stammering before Jah cut him off.

"What the fuck De! When I called yo ass and told you we was bringing Caiden back, what the fuck that mean? We bringin' his lil ass back! Yall nasty bitches up in here fuckin' like you couldn't fuckin' wait. Got dick, ass, pussy, and balls all on my mufuckin counters. Getchall nasty ass on back there to the goddamn room!"

"Where my mommy go? Where her go?" Caiden asked heading towards the kitchen.

"Her naked ass back there hiding," Jah mumbled.

Jazmin heard giggling.

"That shit ain't fuckin funny," Jah snapped.

Now Jazmin couldn't help but release a few giggles of her own. She followed Jah into the living room space while the two love birds continued to get themselves together.

Jazmin whispered to Jah, "Uhm…you know we had sex in my kitchen that one time."

Jah grinned, "We sho in the fuck did. But that was yo house. This ain't they shit."

"You're not gonna let them have it?" Jazmin asked.

"Nope," he answered. He reached for Genesis. "Give me my baby."

Handing Genesis over, she said, "They might as well have this Jah. You're moving back in with me, right?"

"I ain't givin' them shit," he murmured. Genesis smiled at him. "See, Genni agreed."

"Genni just like to hear you talk," Jazmin said. She rolled her eyes and playfully said, "She's gonna enjoy cussing people out too."

"That's Daddy's baby," Jah sang to Genesis causing her to coo back to him.

Gina finally made her way over to where they were sitting. Jazmin could tell she seemed slightly embarrassed but not enough that she was ashamed.

Smoothing out her sundress, Gina took a seat in the chair. She smiled, "So how was he?"

"He was good—" Jazmin was saying before Jah interrupted her.

He glowered at Gina. "If you don't take yo ass and wash the fuck up!"

Surprising to Jazmin, Gina simply waved him off. "Whatever Jah." She looked at Jazmin and smiled, "I'm so glad to be finally talking to you. For a minute I didn't think you liked me."

Jah said, "She didn't like yo ass cause she thought we was fuckin'."

Gina gasped with surprise. "Really?"

Jazmin let out a guilty laugh. "I did."

Turning up her nose with disgust, Gina said, "Oh no! Jah too young for me. Plus he got an awful mouth. I don't see how you can deal with it."

Jazmin wasn't sure if it was her insecurities returning, but she wasn't completely convinced that Gina didn't want Jah. It was something about the way she cut her eyes towards him. It caused Jazmin to glance towards Jah. He was focused on Genesis.

Looking at Gina, it was hard for Jazmin to believe that Jah wouldn't have some type of attraction for her. Gina was very pretty, young and vibrant. She had a gorgeous body that Jazmin was sure turned many men's heads. It left Jazmin in wonderment about how such a young beautiful girl would prefer an older man like Dewalis. It wasn't that Dewalis wasn't attractive; he was the older version of Jah. He was just...old.

Gina looked over at Genesis in Jah's arms and her face brightened with adoration. "Caiden c'mere. I remember when you were this little."

"But I grow big; bigger and bigger," Caiden said emphasizing his ginormous growth with his arms as he walked over.

Gina looked over at Jah and Jazmin sitting next to each other on the sofa. She asked, "Yall having anymore?"

Jazmin hesitated. She looked back at Jah.

He answered, "Not right now."

Internally, Jazmin sighed with relief thankful that he didn't say not ever.

"I guess you gotta wait til your little court thing is handled first, huh?" Gina asked. She didn't wait for a response. Her eyes grew with excitement. "Oh it would be so nice if yall got married. That's what you need to do."

Jah groaned, his irritation evident on his face. He passed Genesis off to Jazmin. Heading towards the kitchen he called out, "C'mere De, lemme holla atchu for a minute."

Jazmin sat there a little crushed that Jah reacted in such a way. He hated the subject of marriage, but she had made it clear it was what she wanted.

"He's such an ass," Gina mumbled.

Jazmin sighed, "I know."

For the next few minutes, Jazmin sat there and listened to Gina rambling on and on about her and Dewalis getting married and she being Jah's stepmother. It wasn't that Jazmin didn't want to like Gina; she just wasn't sure about the girl's intentions. And one thing she wanted to be sure about was the way Jah and Gina related to one another.

Once the visit was over and they were back in her car, Jazmin asked, "How do you feel about Gina?"

"She dumb as hell," Jah stated without much thought as he focused on driving.

"Yeah, but she's really pretty."

"What that gotta do with her being dumb as hell?"

"You don't like her?"

"She aight," he said with a frown.

"Yeah but she's young and got a banging body and—"

"Shut up Juicy," he said shaking his head. "I already know whatchu thinkin' 'bout. I don't want Gina. You know what kinda hoe she is? She one of them ditzy ass broads that prey on old men, sugar daddies. She just didn't know she fucked up when she got with Dewalis ass. Nigga that artificial sugar."

Jazmin snickered. "Okay Jah."

"You always thinkin' I'm thinkin 'bout the next bitch. I ain't no goddamn Sean or that gay mufucka that drive that lil red ass car."

"I know…It's just that…the way she was looking at you. I mean, if yall messed around just tell me."

Jah let out a wry laugh. "Messed around? I know I don't always show Dewalis respect like I should, but to fuck wit his baby mama? Hell naw!"

Jazmin wanted to believe Jah was being honest. The more she thought about it, the more absurd it sound. She should have just remained quiet.

Jah's phone rang and he answered it on speaker. "What nigga?"

"When you coming through today?" Rock asked.

"I don't know. Why? Wassup?"

"Cause I'm tryna do something."

"Impatient ass nigga," Jah murmured under his breath. "I'll be through there in an hour or so."

"Sound like you driving. Where you going to?"

"I just left the condo."

"To holla atcho daddy?"

"Yeah and drop Caiden's bad ass off."

Rock lowered his voice to a sneaky tone. "Did she try to give you that pussy?"

"What!" Jazmin exclaimed in shock.

Jah chuckled, "Goddammit Rock! You fuckin up."

Rock was laughing, "Oh shit! Jazmin witchu?"

"What did you just say Rock?" Jazmin asked.

"Aw…nothin'," Rock mumbled. He sang in the phone, "Hey Jazmin! Whatchu doin' girl?"

"Fuck both of yall!" Jazmin spat. She crossed her arms over her chest and sulked.

"Nigga, you dumb as fuck. Get off my mufuckin' phone," Jah said ending the call. He looked over at Jazmin and couldn't help but laugh. He reached out for her. "Juicy, I know you won't believe me but Gina ain't never tried nothin'. Rock always fuck wit me 'bout that shit."

"Whatever Jah," she murmured. She focused on the traffic outside her window. "You lied to me."

"I just said Rock be fuckin with me. Damn!"

Jazmin didn't say anything else. She thought about her luck with men. They all were liars and had ulterior motives. She wanted to believe that Jah had a genuine love for her or maybe she was just desperate to be loved and she was settling for Jah. Whatever the case, she didn't have much time to figure all of this out with him.

———

It felt weird, but Sean was glad he had his wires removed. He could talk normal again but he had to remind himself to steer clear of Jabari Bradford. If there was one lesson that he could take away from the entire situation was to never cross Jah. That was something he should have known anyway. Jah had always shown who he was; what made Sean believe he would take it easy on him?

The only thing—well two things that Sean regretted was having a child with Erica that she ultimately left on him to care for and losing Jazmin. He knew she should be the furthest thing from his mind, but he did miss her. Of all the women he messed around with on the side, he could honestly say that Jazmin had claimed a spot in his heart. Thinking back on it, he felt bad for the way he treated her. She wasn't deserving of it. She certainly was deserving of more than being with Jah though. It was just hard to imagine Jazmin being seriously involved with him. But Genesis existence was the evidence of that.

He had taken Jazmin's love for him for granted. He made the mistake in thinking that she would always be there. All it took was one moment of negligence and another man was able to come along and get inside. Though Jah's presence in heart lay dormant, Sean's selfishness was the catalyst to make it manifest.

Snapping him out of his thought, Rayven said, "Now that you're just about healed, it's time that you move out and get you and DeSean a place to stay."

"But I thought we were living here," he replied.

"I said until you healed and got better," she reminded. She let them inside their home. The three of them had just came back from Sean's doctor's appointment.

"I know what you said, but I thought things between us were better."

"I'm hungry," DeSean interjected.

Rayven headed up the stairs, "Make your son something to eat."

Sean looked at DeSean staring back at him with big eyes. "What do you want?"

DeSean followed Sean into the kitchen, "Uhm...A happy meal!"

"No happy meals," Sean said over his shoulders.

"A cheeseburger and nuggets," DeSean suggested with hope.

"No happy meals," Sean repeated. He started rummaging through the refrigerator and cabinets. Since he had been back home with Rayven and DeSean, she had been caring for both him and his son. She seemed to enjoy doing so, but now that he was almost one hundred percent better, she was being flippant again.

Sean settled on making DeSean a ham and cheese sandwich. After situating his son at the kitchen table, Sean made his way upstairs to join Rayven. She was lying on their bed flipping through the channels on the television.

Sean asked, "So what was the other night Rayven?"

"The sex we had?" she asked with hilarity.

"Yeah."

"That was nothing," she said nonchalantly.

"Nothing huh?" Sean asked with thought as he made his way to the bed.

Settling on the Oxygen channel, Rayven said with a cynical grin, "Well look at that; a *Snapped* marathon."

Ignoring Rayven's innuendo, Sean said, "Ray, you can't continue to be mad at me forever. For the past couple of weeks, things have been okay between us."

"Because I don't care anymore. I only let the two of you stay out of the kindness of my heart. But you're better and you should be gathering your things."

"So is this what you're becoming now? Some heartless bitch?" he asked with his nose turned up in disdain.

"You've got your nerves. And if I've become this way, it's because of the shit you've thrown my way. I'm so done over you Sean. Just be grateful that I've allowed you here this long."

"Allowed? This is my house just as much as it yours."

"A court won't see it that way after I enter evidence of your infidelities."

Sean looked at her protruding belly. Rayven was a little less than seven months pregnant. She would need him. He couldn't understand why she was being so stubborn. He decided to use that as leverage.

"What about the baby?"

"What about it?" she countered.

"I wanna be here for my baby, our baby."

"We don't have to be together because of the baby Sean," she stated.

"Rayven, will you stop!" Sean snapped. He was beyond frustrated with her unbending stance.

"Stop what?" she asked. She folded her arms over her chest and stared at him hard. "When will you stop popping your dick in every chick that walks by?"

"It isn't like that."

"You could have fooled me."

"It isn't. I admitted to you I was a little fucked up. I also said that we could work through this. We were starting counseling Ray."

"Sean, you basically admitted that you loved Jazmin. Do you still?"

Without hesitation, he lied, "No. Jazmin was just there when you and I weren't on good terms. She came on to me. She made it easy Ray."

"What about Sabrina, Michelle, and Erica?"

"I wasn't fucking with them like that. Okay, I had a moment—a one night of bad decision making. Me and Rock...and Michelle and Sabrina. And DeSean was before we got married."

Rayven rolled her eyes shaking her head. "We were still dating Sean. And Erica hinted at you two still messing around with each other. After all, isn't that why Jah pummeled your ass?"

"No," Sean shook his head emphatically. "No, no, no...Jah did what he did because he's Jah. I was over there seeing DeSean when Jah showed up. I mean, yeah, I'm sorry for keeping DeSean a secret but I was afraid that we would end up where we are now. I know I fucked up Ray but being with you is what I truly want. I don't expect us to resolve all of our issues and be perfect overnight, but I'm willing to give it my all. Being here with you, DeSean, and our baby boy is what I need Ray."

Rayven's heart soften a smidgen. The idea of raising their baby alone wasn't appealing at all to Rayven. Deep down inside, she did want to forgive Sean and move on. But a part of her, felt ashamed for taking him back. Then again, the ones that would have the most to say weren't her friends anymore anyway. That thought sadden her. She did miss Desiree but things were as they were now.

"I tell you what," Rayven started. She gave it more thought before she continued, "You and DeSean can stay here. I'm not ready for you to move back in here with me though. You continue to sleep in the guest room. We'll work on us one issue at a time, one day at a time."

Sean smiled. That's what he needed to hear. Mission accomplished here. Now he just had to figure out a way to keep Michelle pacified.

Chapter 12

Jazmin knew she was the most hardheaded woman alive. She knew she was going against what her good friend Landrus had told her: Do not confront Lamar alone. But Jazmin couldn't risk Jah finding out. It was bad enough he was battling charges with the whole Sean and Erica situation. A murder charge for Lamar would put Jah away forever. Besides, her knowledge about what happened was eating at her. She had to confront Lamar.

As she stood outside of Lamar's apartment door, she could hear music coming from the other side. She found that strange because Lamar was usually a very reserved individual and wouldn't play loud music like that in the middle of the day.

Knocking on the door as hard as she could, Jazmin became nervous. What would she say exactly? What if he denied everything? What if he tried to make her seem crazy?

After no answer and music still blaring, Jazmin pounded on the door again. Seconds later the music lowered and she could hear footsteps nearing the door.

The door swung open and Jazmin was hit with two things: the smell of something good cooking and the person at the door was not Lamar.

"How can I help you?" the Asian lady asked.

Jazmin took in the sight of the model thin flawlessly made up to perfection woman standing at an average height. This woman was beautiful. She stared back at Jazmin fluttering her long showy eyelashes with her gold bangled hand rested on her slim hip.

"I was looking for Lamar. Is he here?" Jazmin asked.

"Oh yeah, he's here. May I ask who you are so I can let him know?"

"Could you tell him it's Jazmin?"

The lady's face lit up with a grin. "Jazmin? You're Jazmin?"

Jazmin was confused. She frowned, "Should I know you?"

"I'm Kyomi, Lamar's fiancée," she said as if Jazmin should know.

Jazmin gave her an uncertain look.

Kyomi ushered Jazmin in. "Oh come on in. Lamar has told me all about you."

"He has?" Jazmin asked as she stepped inside the apartment's living room area.

"Yes," Kyomi stated. She looked Jazmin up and down. "He said you were pretty. Now are all of the women in your family on the heavy side or is it just you?"

Jazmin was taken aback by the blatant rudeness. "Excuse me?"

"Well I was just asking because we'd have to consider the genes in our baby's blood. Is the hair yours?"

Frowning, Jazmin was completely thrown off. "Yes the hair is mine. Where is Lamar?"

"He's freshening up. I'll go get him," Kyomi said. She gave Jazmin another excited grin. "I'm just so happy you're doing this for us."

As Kyomi dashed off, Jazmin called out to her, "What am I doing?"

Of course her question was left unanswered. When Lamar followed Kyomi back into the living room, Jazmin's mood soured just by his sight. He stared at her trying to read her and she stared back at him coldly.

Nervously, Lamar rubbed the back of his neck. "Jazmin, what are you doing over here?"

"I came to talk to you about something important," she replied.

Kyomi's face sadden. With a pout she asked, "It's not about the baby is it? You're still going to do it for us, right?"

Jazmin's mouth hung open unable to form any words. She looked from Kyomi to Lamar.

Lamar looked down at Kyomi and asked softly, "Hey, can I speak with Jazmin alone? Just for a sec."

Kyomi looked worried as she glanced towards Jazmin. She nodded. "I got to check on the food anyway."

After Kyomi sashayed away in her platform pumps, Jazmin asked, "What's going on?"

"Uhm," he started uneasily. "That's Kyomi."

"She said she was your fiancée."

"Well...she is."

Jazmin was floored. "Are you fucking serious? How long has she been your fiancée Lamar?"

"Look Jazmin, none of that really matter. You're with Jah now. Let me be with Kyomi."

Jazmin laughed angrily. "Do you hear yourself? You're talking as if I've been hounding you pushing the idea of an 'us' on you! I don't care who you're with. I'm just trying to figure out why you were lying."

Lamar glanced over in Kyomi's direction who was trying to listen to the conversation. He said, "I tried to tell you this wasn't about us. I thought you understood that. If I had known, I wouldn't have asked you to do this."

Jazmin was even more confused and pissed. "What the fuck are you talking about Lamar? You have some serious issues. You're fucking sick in the head!"

"I see you've been hanging around Jah a lot."

Kyomi walked back over. She asked Lamar, "Is she not going to do it now?"

"Do what!" Jazmin exclaimed angrily.

"Jazmin, calm down," Lamar said soothingly. "We can talk this over like adults."

Kyomi was genuinely confused also. "What's the problem baby?"

Lamar eyed Jazmin as he spoke, "She doesn't want to do it unless she and I are together."

Kyomi turned to Jazmin, "Oh no, you can't have my husband-to-be. He thought you were a good fit to have our baby but if he thought you would have taken it the wrong way, he never would have asked you. And I understand you may be upset, but I'm still willing to pay you to be our surrogate and donor."

Jazmin could only see red. In seconds it took her to realize what was going on. It took the same seconds to reach for the nearest object and try to beat Lamar with it. In a matter of minutes with all of the scuffling, Lamar's living room looked like a mild earthquake shook it up.

"Get out!" Kyomi screamed.

With her hair ruffled and out of breath, Jazmin glared at Lamar. "I'm getting out you fucking baby killer! Yeah, I know what you did Lamar! That's why I came over here. So you enjoy Ling Ling and all of your baby hunting while you can. I'm gonna get somebody to fuck you up!"

"What are you talking about!" Lamar shot back.

"Fuck you! Keep standing there thinking I'm stupid. I know you caused me to have my miscarriage. And when—"

"Miscarriage?" Kyomi asked in disbelief. "Why would you do that Lamar? What did you do?"

"I didn't do anything. She's delusional," Lamar stated.

"We'll see how delusional I am when you get your ass beat!" Jazmin said before storming out of the apartment. Before she even got to her car she had pulled her phone out. She made a phone call.

237

It went straight to voicemail. She left a message, "This is Jazmin. Please call me when you get this. It's about that Lamar situation...I think I'm ready to handle it. So please call me so we can discuss this."

———

As Jah pulled up to his aunt's house, he witnessed Tyrell pulling out of Nivea's driveway in her car. He shook his heads in pity and utter disgust. Nivea was none of his business, but it amazed him how she talked all of that shit about Tyrell, yet the nigga was driving her car around and Jah was sure he was living there too.

Getting out of the car, he could feel Nivea's eyes on him. He hoped she didn't get the idea to walk over and try to talk to him. He wasn't really in the mood for her ass; not today.

Ignoring her, Jah opened the back door of his new SUV to retrieve Genesis in her carseat. She was still asleep. Before he could make it to the door, Georgia was already standing there reaching for Genesis.

"Where them dogs at?" Georgia asked.

"They in the car. I think they think I'm finna carry they asses in here," Jah chuckled.

"You know your sister had them spoiled like that," Georgia laughed.

"And Juicy tryna spoil they asses now," Jah said heading back to his vehicle. He opened the passenger side door and grabbed Genesis' bag. He then ushered Mittenz and Sox to get out of the car. They looked out onto the ground and then back up at him.

"If yall don't getchall monkey asses out of my shit! Bring yall asses on!"

Georgia was laughing. "You can't call the dogs monkeys Jah!"

Mittenz and Sox finally hopped out of the car and scurried towards the door.

"Them lil mufuckas gon be whateva the fuck I call they ass." He followed Georgia inside the house but he didn't go far. He sat Genesis' bag on the living room sofa. "You good?"

"I'm fine," Georgia said waving him off. "You take care of Jazmin."

"I'ma try. She actin' all funny and shit."

"Just take her out and try to show her a good time. What did you do to her anyway?"

Shaking his head and lightly smiling, he said, "Nothing Auntie. She a woman and you know how yall do."

"Naw! It ain't no 'you know how yall do'. Yall men have a way of doing shit to us and when we don't respond in a way you're willing to tolerate then it's us with the damn problem. We crazy. Your Uncle Leon be trying that shit with me."

"Whateva. Yall mufuckin crazy," Jah joked. "But anyway, I gotta go. Love ya Auntie."

"Yall be careful," Georgia called after him. She stood in the doorway and smiled. "Look atchu nephew. This your new ride?"

"Yeah," Jah beamed proudly.

"What Jazmin say?"

"She don't know it's mine."

Georgia saw someone approaching from the corner of her eye. She turned her head and her smile faded. Her lips twisted up with a look of skepticism and disdain. She cut her eyes at Nivea. She then looked at Jah, "Don't be forever getting 'way from here boy."

"Aight," Jah said. He waited until Georgia had retreated all the way in her house before addressing Nivea. "What's up?"

Nivea scoffed in amusement. "Your aunt hates me now, huh?"

"I wouldn't say hate. She just don't like yo ass."

Nivea walked up on him and his truck. With her hands on both hips and admiring the shine of the new SUV, she said, "Is this your new vehicle?"

"Yeah."

"When you gonna take me riding in it?"

"Never," he answered. He hopped in the driver's seat but left the door open.

"You still mad at me?"

"Why the fuck you come over here?"

"To see if we could patch things up between us."

Jah chuckled genuinely amused. "Nivea, get the fuck on. I got somewhere to be."

"Wait Jah," she said. She lowered her eyes and spoke nervously, "I think I might need your help with my situation."

"Waiting on me to help you then you fucked," Jah told her. He reached for his door but she stepped inside the door preventing him from closing it.

"Jah, seriously. I need to get rid of Tee. He won't leave. Can you help me?"

"Hell naw! That's yo shit," Jah said. "Now can yo ass move so I can fuckin' go?"

"Jah!"

"Sorry but I can't help you," was all he could offer her.

"Really Jah?" she said in disbelief.

"Really Niv. Unless yo name is Jazmin or Genesis, I can't do shit for ya," he said. He pushed her just enough to move her out of his door's way. He closed the door and said, "Keep yo head up ma; it'll get better."

Nivea rolled her eyes and gave him the finger.

"Aight, fuck you too then," Jah told her as he backed up. The last thing he needed to do was get himself caught up in another mess. He was already facing the possibility of being gone from Jazmin and Genesis' lives. He didn't need more charges and time added to what he was facing. And anything involving Tyrell would sure to do just that.

———

Jazmin wasn't sure if she was still up to going out that night. She wasn't feeling the best physically or emotionally. She was nauseous and lately she had been really stressed. There was the Lamar situation of course. Then there was the not knowing of Jah's fate. His lawyer had a court date set for a discussion to possibly get the DA to have the charges dropped. And there was just Jah himself.

Sometimes, Jazmin wasn't sure how to take him. He was so nonchalant about things. He didn't make a big deal about the things she worried about and the things she didn't worry about he made a big deal of. Things were different this time than it was when he first came to live with her after she had given birth to Genesis. The vibe was different. It wasn't bad; it was just intense. There seemed to be more invested and more at stake this time around. The first time, Jah was just there and they were pretending. This time, it was real. They were in a real relationship trying to make things work. He still got on her nerves. He still left a trail of mess wherever he went in the house. And he still didn't care.

The past two weeks they fell into routine. Adjusting was effortless. Jah was working back with her father regularly. She worked out a deal with BevyCo to do her work remotely. Being a close relative of those in charge had its benefits which she absolutely loved. She was able to work, keep a consistent eye on Genesis, and still gossip on the phone all day.

She was still leery of that phone conversation Jah and Rock had about Gina. Jah tried to assure her it was all a joke. She wanted to believe him but remembering how most men were, she wasn't able to fully believe him. He swore on his mother and Sheena that he didn't want Gina. That was the only thing that allowed Jazmin to overlook it for the time being. However he thought she wasn't being very communicative because of that. It wasn't that at all. It was everything unknown.

The alarm system chimed indicating the door had been opened. Jazmin didn't bother to get up from the sofa. When Jah came into view she just stared at him.

"C'mon. You ready?" he asked.

"I don't wanna go anywhere," she murmured.

"Yeah you do. Cause yo ass finna be complaining next week 'bout'chu never getting to go nowhere. So bring yo ass on!"

"Jah, you go out. I'll be fine here," she said.

Jah walked over to where she sat until he stood in front of her. He grabbed both of her hands in his to pull her up. "C'mon juicy booty. Cassie and Rock out there anyway."

"They are?" she asked as she allowed him to pull her to her feet.

"Cassie gon come in here and beatcho ass if I tell her you ain't goin."

"She'll understand," Jazmin said with little enthusiasm.

"What's wrong?" Jah asked her seriously. He pulled her into him and wrapped his arms around her.

"I'm not in a really good mood."

"Are you still worried 'bout that shit Rock said on the phone?"

She shook her head. "No but I wouldn't trust you and Gina alone."

"I almost threw yo ass," Jah said playfully.

Jazmin chuckled, "You bet not."

"Man, I wish you let that shit go. Rock even told you he was just playin'."

"Yeah but you two are supposed to cover up for each other," Jazmin pointed out. "But I'm not as bothered by that anymore."

"What is it then? Do I need to beat somebody's ass?"

She shook her head. "No."

The door sounded off. Cassie's voice could be heard before she was seen. "Where you at Jazz!"

"Here come crazy," Jah whispered to Jazmin.

She pulled away from him and grabbed her purse from the sofa just as Cassie stepped into the den. Her whole demeanor changed and she seemed thrilled to see Cassie.

Cassie grinned at Jazmin. "Look at you! Looking like yo shit don't stink!"

Jazmin smiled as she joined her friend. "You're looking cute too."

Jah stared at Jazmin trying to figure out why he couldn't get this same energetic reaction out of her. It was clear to him that her bothered state was because of something he did. What he done exactly was a mystery to him.

By the time they stepped outside and Jah locked up the house, he had developed an attitude.

Getting in the backseat of Jah's Caprice confused Jazmin. She looked at the shiny bronze Yukon Denali sitting in her driveway wondering who it belonged to. She looked over at Jah sitting next to her and asked, "Why is Rock driving?"

"Ask him," was all Jah said.

"Who's truck out there?" Jazmin asked.

"That's your hubby's truck," Caprice said excitedly from the front seat. "He sold Rock this car. You didn't know?"

Jazmin's mouth dropped open. She turned to face Jah. She smiled, "You didn't tell me you were doing that."

He shrugged.

"Why did you do that?"

"I wanted something more family like and Rock's ass needed a car."

Jazmin's heart warmed. That was a very kind and thoughtful thing for Jah to do. But then again, Jah was always kind and thoughtful on the inside. In that moment, Jazmin had to really sit on that revelation and appreciate that about Jah.

"That was nice of you Jah," she said. She snuggled up beside him and rested her head on his shoulder. Her hand slithered under his shirt as she hugged him close.

Jah smiled on the inside. That was something he had grown to anticipate with Jazmin. She could never just be satisfied with being next to him or lying next to him. Somehow she had to make their skin touch. Jah wasn't even sure she was aware of what she did but for him it signified her desire to be one with him. But if that was the case, why did it seem like she was shutting him out...again?

Then there was her persistent nagging about marriage. He wouldn't call it nagging exactly, but when he heard it all of the time that's what it became. The idea of marriage always bothered Jah yet it was something he wished he was made for. Being able to love just one woman for the rest of his life wasn't what he feared. He felt he was more than capable of doing that especially when it came to the love of his life, Jazmin. Now that they shared a child, it only seemed more desirable. However, he couldn't stand the idea of vowing to be some woman's husband and then failing her.

Jazmin wanted to get married to solidify their relationship but he still wasn't sure about the outcome of his charges. On top of that, they hadn't really just tried to live with one another as a couple as they were now. It had only been a couple of weeks and it seemed as though Jazmin wasn't so sure about things anymore. Since she heard Rock saying that bullshit over the phone about Gina, Jazmin pushed it on him even more. But if Jah was confident and sure of himself and sure of what he could bring to the table, he would marry Jazmin. He would marry her not only because he loved the hell out of her but because if Sheena and his mother were alive, they would want it. They would want Jah to be happy and for him to have what was best for him. Settling down and having a family of his own would definitely steer him or should steer him clear of the streets. Now it made sense what Abe was trying to do for him. Having a family that depended on him would give him purpose. Being able to meet their needs and fulfill his purpose would be more rewarding at the end of the day.

Sheena always reminded him that life was too short. If Sheena had had more time, she would have married Brian and had some bad ass little biracial kids. She would definitely be encouraging him to get Jazmin the ring she adored. He didn't even know what that was.

Jah wrapped his arm around Jazmin and kissed the top of her head. "I love you juicy booty."

Jazmin smiled and turned her face up to look at him. They shared a sweet peck of the lips. She said, "I love you too."

———

Later that night, Jazmin found herself in such a better mood than she had been before. She also noticed that Jah had loosen up. They were good. And if felt good. They actually were enjoying one another as a couple alongside Cassie and Rock. Compared to those two, their relationship was lovey dovey.

"You just be glad I'm giving your ass another chance," Cassie said rolling her eyes at Rock.

"Don't show out," Rock warned.

"Who showing out?" Cassie said. She focused all of her attention to the menu before her.

"You nigga," Rock said. "Talkin' 'bout giving me another chance. You know you don't want me goin' nowhere."

"Whatever," she said dismissively. "I didn't ask you to —"

"Lie again," Rock interrupted.

"Rock just shut up and figure out whatcho stupid ass wanna eat," Cassie frowned.

Rock laughed and leaned in to kiss her. She tried to act uninterested but a smile crept across her face as she kissed him.

Jazmin grinned. "Aren't they cute baby?"

"They stupid as hell," Jah mumbled as he studied the menu. He asked, "And why did we end up at this mufuckin' place?"

"Cause it's the only shit I could afford nigga," Rock joked. "What the fuck you mean? I ain't ballin' like yo ass buying twenty-fifteen trucks and shit."

"That's a two thousand fifteen?" Jazmin asked Jah.

"Yeah," Jah answered. He looked across the table at Rock and gave him a teasing smile. "But'chu 'bout to nigga so shut the fuck up."

Cassie's head whipped up at full attention. "What that mean?"

"Look at her," Rock nodded his head towards Cassie. "Money hungry ass."

"I'm not," she said. "I just wanna know what Jah mean by that. You the one that got all these kids and baby mamas. It would be nice to know that you can take care of them with no problems."

"Naw, it'd be nice to know that I can take care of them and still get you every fuckin thing you want. Cassie, you think you slick," Rock told her.

Cassie rolled her eyes upwards. "Whatever Rodney Jamison."

"What I told you 'bout that?" Rock asked. "Don't be speaking out loud my gov'ment like that."

Cassie laughed. "You swear like you somebody important!"

"I am," Rock said. He nodded his head with a knowing smirk. He winked at Jazmin. "Your boy just got into Bevy."

It was Jazmin's time to be amused. "What?"

Jah shot Rock a look. "Shut up nigga. I told Abe not to put'cho simple ass on. You gon fuck shit up for everybody."

Cassie frowned up with suspicion. She asked Jazmin, "What they talkin' about?"

Jazmin looked from Jah to Rock with her own suspicions. "I don't know but I'ma find out. Bevy is Lu's company. What do you mean by Abe putting Rock on?"

"It's nothin'," Jah said. He looked around, "Where that bitch at so we can order this weak ass food."

Cassie said, "Jah, ain't nothin' wrong with O'Charley's. It's still food."

"Nigga done ate a couple of fancy places with Abe an'nem and now he too good for O'Charley's," Rock teased.

"Fuck you nigga," Jah muttered.

Jazmin interjected, "Well, we failed to make reservations anywhere else and all the better places have long wait times. It was either this or McDonald's or Pizza Hut."

Just then their waitress came over with pen and pad ready to take their orders. After Jah gave her his entrée order she asked, "Soup or salad?"

Jah's brow furrowed into a scowl. As if the waitress wasn't standing there, he looked at Rock and asked, "What the fuck she say?"

"Soup or salad?" the waitress repeated.

Rock gave Jah the same confused look. They both asked at the same time, "What the fuck is a super salad?"

Jazmin covered her face with her menu to block her laughter.

Cassie started clowning them. "She didn't say no damn super salad. Yall both dumb as hell. She said *soup* or *salad*."

"Aw!" Rock laughed.

"I thought the mufuckin salad had super powers or some shit," Jah chuckled.

Jazmin was too tickled to even place her order. She had to make Jah move so that she could get out of the booth to go use the restroom before she had an accident.

Cassie decided to join Jazmin. After they handled their business in the lady's room, they made their way back to their area of the restaurant. While weaving in and out of the tables, a couple caught Jazmin's attention.

Before Jazmin could say anything, Cassie asked, "Ay...ain't that Lamar? Who is that he with?"

"It is Lamar," Jazmin said lowly. She continued to walk towards their area. Cassie was walking behind her but was still trying to be nosey.

"What the fuck is that with him?" Cassie asked with her nose turned up.

"That's his fiancée, Kyomi," Jazmin answered.

"Fiancée? Since when?"

Jazmin shrugged. As they approached their table, both Rock and Jah got up so that the ladies could slide back in the booth.

"Ooh yall! Guess who in here?" Cassie couldn't wait to talk about what she saw.

"Who?" Rock asked.

"Look over there," Cassie directed. She pointed in the direction where Lamar was seated. From where they were, they had a good side view of Lamar and Kyomi.

"Who is that?" Rock asked.

"Gay boy," Jah mumbled.

Kyomi got up with her clutch purse in hand and twitched away towards the bathroom.

"I told yo ass!" Jah said with a little too much excitement.

"Told me what?" Jazmin asked.

"That mufucka is gay. Why he on a date wit a fuckin' dude?"

Jazmin was confused. "That's not a guy Jah."

"You dumb as hell if you think that was a woman. That's a nigga!" Jah told her.

Cassie and Rock were cracking up.

"Jah, I seen the girl up close," Jazmin argued.

"Juicy, you don't pay attention to everything. You be seeing only the shit you wanna see," Jah said to her. "Watch when that mufucka come back. As a matter of fact, I'll be back."

"Jah!" Jazmin called out to him as he got up. She lowered her head and closed her eyes saying a small prayer. "Please God don't let this man act a fool up in here. Not tonight."

Cassie said, "That's why I asked what was that. She looked a lil suspect to me too Jazz."

Jazmin kept her eyes on Jah as she watched him approach Lamar at his table. She wished she could make out what was being said. One thing was for sure, Lamar looked spooked upon seeing Jah. There was a moment when both of them looked back over at the table where they were seated.

"That nigga look nervous," Rock noted. "He can't deny being with that it. We see his ass."

Kyomi returned to the table and was a bit surprised to see that they had a visitor. Some words were exchanged between Kyomi and Jah.

Lamar became very uncomfortable. Kyomi sat down and looked to Lamar. Jah turned away and headed back to the table.

Kyomi and Lamar seemed to be arguing now. Jazmin could only imagine what Jah could have said.

"What happened Jah?" Cassie asked.

Jah sat down and stared at Jazmin. "You know that's a goddamn man right?"

Jazmin chuckled. "Why do you say that? What did you say to them anyway? They over there arguing."

"I don't know what the fuck they arguin' 'bout, but I know that's a mufuckin man," Jah said. "Look at her shoulders and shit. I know you seen that mothafuckin big ass Adam's apple on that bitch throat."

Jazmin looked over at the couple. The day she confronted Lamar, she must have been too shocked to really notice the details. Kyomi was wearing a strapless blouse exposing her rather squared shoulders and muscular biceps. Looking at Kyomi's face, she could see how angular her facial structure was. Then combine it all with the fact that Kyomi thought Jazmin was going to be their surrogate and donor. *Well, I'll be damn!* Jazmin thought.

"That gay mufucka tried to deny it until that other nigga showed up all proud and shit. I asked it was it a man or woman and the bitch said, 'why do it matter'. I got my fuckin' answer ol' faggoty asses," Jah said as if he was disgusted.

"You just went over there and interrupted their nice evening out," Cassie said.

"I don't give a fuck. I told it to keep its mufuckin man away from my Juicy too. Don't nobody want his bald headed ass but that over there. Ol dick in the booty ass niggas."

Jazmin continued to stare at Lamar. He was even sicker than she thought. The fact that he was still out and about irritated Jazmin but she knew it was only a matter of time before Lamar was getting his.

———

"Guess who's back together?"

"Who?" Jazmin asked as she handed Cassie fresh towels and washcloths. It had gotten late and both Jah and Rock had too much to drink. Jazmin suggested that Cassie and Rock crash at her place.

Tanya said, "Ray and Sean."

"Are you serious?" Jazmin asked in disbelief.

"I'm dead serious. And he got his lil boy now."

"What little boy?"

"You know. The one with Erica."

"Oh really?"

"You know Erica left the lil boy with them and her ass ain't nowhere to be found."

"Well the boy is probably better off. I just can't believe Rayven gave in and took Sean back. How do you know this anyway?"

"I've got my sources," Tanya chuckled.

"Yeah, usually it's Cassie with all the news."

Tanya snorted a laugh. "Yeah until she started getting dick on a regular basis. Tell that bitch I miss her ass. She been missing in action and shit."

"I'll tell her," Jazmin said making her way into her bedroom. She pushed the door closed. She asked, "So who is this source?"

"I ain't tellin'."

"Aw c'mon Tanya. I thought we weren't keeping secrets anymore."

"Who said that? I didn't say that."

"Who is it?"

"Somebody that talk to Sean on a regular basis. Aw yeah, they told me about your sister and

Damien getting back together too. All yall bitches been missing in action; laying up and shit."

"Well what's going on with you and Tyrell?"

Tanya's tone changed. "Fuck that nigga."

"Yall not on good terms anymore?"

"I don't think we ever was," Tanya said sadly at her revelation. "Once he found out that Jah's aunt lived next to Nivea, he said to hell with me and Tyriq."

"Are you serious? Jah isn't even at Georgia's house; he's here."

"I know that but that nigga insecure and wanna control shit," Tanya pointed out. "He thought he was gon' pop up in and out over here but I wasn't with the shit. I mean, I had a weak moment where I believed in his ass. I was just happy that he was out and we could actually have a real relationship this time around. But fuck that. He ain't about shit. And it took somebody else to break it down for me."

"Who?"

Tanya started taunted her playfully. "Now see, you keep being nosey. In due time...in due time."

Jazmin heard the shower starting. "Well, let me go. I guess I'll come over there tomorrow while Genni is still gone."

"Aight. I'll be here," Tanya said before ending the call.

Jazmin tossed her phone on her bed and she headed for the bathroom. She quickly undressed and twisted her hair up into a tight bun. She welcomed herself into the shower with Jah. Before he could turn around and notice her she walked up behind him and wrapped her arms around him and placed her head on his back.

No need for an exchange of words; they just stood there relishing the moment. As always, Jazmin enjoyed her day with Jah. He could be a bit much at times, but he was who he was; love him or hate him. Loving him was easy and that's what she knew was the scariest. Being involved with Sean presented a challenge or so she thought. She had to win Sean over. She had to convince him that she was just as good as Rayven when in actuality he didn't really care. She was just another convenient piece of ass. With Jah, she got to be herself. He made her feel comfortable even in her nakedness. She had no choice really because he wouldn't let her cover up.

Jah turned around in her arms and pulled her closer in his embrace. She looked up at him and smiled.

"You goofy," he told her.

"I know," she grinned. She lifted on her toes to plant a kiss on his lips. She could still taste the alcohol. She asked, "Can we have sex in the shower?"

Jah frowned, "What the fuck wrong wit you? You been wantin to fuck more than me. Ever since I been here yo ass been jumpin on my dick every chance you get."

She giggled. "I don't know."

"You pregnant aint'chu?"

"Why do you think that's the reason for everything?"

"You didn't drink nothin' earlier. Yo ass horny than a mothafucka. Pussy stay hot. You moody as fuck. And yo stomach still hard."

"You're moody too!" she argued playfully. "Are you pregnant? You couldn't even hold your liquor. Who you got pregnant Jah?"

"You nigga!" he exclaimed. Then he said to her seriously, "You told me you had a miscarriage though."

Jazmin pulled away from him and looked away guiltily. "I did."

"So why you lookin like that?"

She shrugged.

"You want anotha baby?"

Her eyes shifted back to his. She answered, "We can't right?"

"Not until after this shit over with."

Moody wasn't exactly what Jazmin was. Every day she had to wrestle with her emotions and force herself not to cry over the smallest things such as this moment. Her feelings felt bruised because he shut the idea of having another baby down. First it was the marriage issue and now no babies.

She avoided eye contact with him as she stepped around him to grab her shower gel and mesh pouf.

"There you go with that poutin shit," Jah said, his annoyance evident in his tone.

"I'm not pouting," she said as she continued to lather her body.

"Give me this shit," he said while snatching the pouf from her.

She rolled her eyes and sighed. "Jah, just give it back so I can get out."

"Lemme wash you," he said.

The scowl on his face was in contrast to the delicate way he handled her body. It was one of those things that made Jazmin smile on the inside and love the man before her.

Jazmin looked at him with remorse in her eyes. There were things she needed to tell him but she was unsure of his reactions. She didn't want him to be upset with her either. He would be mad either way, more so that she kept this information from him.

The feel of his lil man growing and poking her put a smile on her face. She looked down and asked, "What's up with that Jah?"

"You already know what's up Juicy. Don't play dumb. I'm 'bout to stick it in you."

Jazmin started laughing. She grabbed her pouf back from him. "You so nasty!"

"Shut up and turn yo ass around and hug the goddamn wall."

Chapter 13

Just as she said she was, Jazmin decided to pay her friend Tanya a visit. Tanya was right; they hadn't been spending as much time together as they used to. Cassie was all into Rock although she tried to maintain a hard, uncaring façade when it came to him. Everybody could see right through it, even Rock himself.

Jazmin knew it would only be a matter of time before Lamar started blowing her phone up. She let him sweat long enough and decided to answer the phone.

Tanya threw her a stern look and gritted, "Don't answer the damn phone!"

Jazmin chuckled and said into the phone, "Hello?"

"Jazz! Don't hang up. Just listen to me."

"I answered the phone Lamar. What do you want? Why are you even calling me?"

He released a heavy frustrated and nervous breath. He said, "I'm sorry I led you on about wanting to be with you. I also didn't want you to find out about Kyomi that way—"

Before he could continue, Jazmin interrupted him. "Lamar, is this another one of your pitiful fronts for Kyomi. Is she there with you or something? Because you're making it seem as if I'm devastated over you and you know that is not the case."

"No, this isn't about her exactly."

"Well what is it?"

"What you said when you came to my apartment that day...what were you trying to say Jazmin? Are you saying that I had something to do with your miscarriage?"

"You had everything to do with it Lamar!" Jazmin screamed angrily. "Landrus didn't know you had made up that lie. He told me. We put two and two together. You did it!"

"Landrus thinks I did that?"

"He's for sure you did it!"

Lamar murmured something under his breath.

"Why?" Jazmin asked.

"What did Landrus say?"

"Why are you worried about that? I wanna know why you did that to me? You know what? It doesn't matter. Once I tell my daddy, my cousins, and Jah, you're dead anyway."

"W-w-w-wait now! Don't go telling anybody anything Jazz. You don't even have concrete proof that I did that."

"All I need is Landrus to back me up," she said. She looked over at a puzzled Tanya. She gestured towards Tanya to get her things so that they could go.

"There's no proof that I did that though!"

"Well everything is such a big fucking coincidence."

"Jazmin, let's try to be rational about all of this. How about we agree to just stay out of each other's lives. I won't bother you and you won't bother me."

Jazmin scoffed as she scooped up her keys and purse. "Is that what you think we should do Lamar? I mean I lost a baby. It was an emotional experience. And then you had the nerves to come around and act as if you were concern. Jah has been so right about you. You're a selfish gay booty chasing bald headed fuck nigga that drives a little ass red car!"

Tanya snickered quietly as she disappeared down her hallway.

"I'm not gay," he firmly disputed.

"Kyomi is not a biological woman, is she?"

"She's just as every bit of a woman as you are."

Tanya returned with Tyriq in tow. Jazmin headed out of Tanya's apartment with the two of them following.

"So now you're a *delusional* selfish gay booty chasing bald headed fuck nigga that drives a little ass red car!" Jazmine was peeved. She found herself lava hot the more she listened to his nonsense.

Tanya didn't know what was going on but she followed Jazmin to her car. She and Tyriq got in while Jazmin continued to talk on the phone.

Trying to play on Jazmin's softer side, Lamar said with feigned defeat and devastation, "Okay, I lied about wanting to be with you. I'll admit that. Kyomi wanted a baby. I thought I could ask you to do this for me so that she and I wouldn't have to go through the whole ordeal of going to an agency. I didn't expect you to be caught up in all of these love affairs though. So I lied."

Jazmin strapped up in her seatbelt. "And you're saying that as if it's okay Lamar! You don't go around doing what you did to me to people. I should have you arrested!"

"I didn't do anything Jazz," he said insistent on his innocence.

Jazmin put the phone on speakerphone so that she could go to her messages. She wrote a text and sent it off.

"What are you doing? Are you texting?" Lamar asked.

"Who I'm texting should be the least of your worries," Jazmin snapped. "Where are you and can you meet with me? We need a face to face. I wanna look you in your eyes when you tell me you didn't do it."

"Jazmin, that's not really —"

"You owe me that! At the least!" Jazmin shouted furiously.

Tanya was a little shocked. She had never seen Jazmin get so mad. She had to know what was going on.

"I'm home but Kyomi will be back soon."

Calming down, Jazmin said, "I won't be long. I just need this so I can put it behind me."

Somewhat relieved Lamar said, "So I take it this will stay between us."

"Lamar, what you did was hurtful. It was also very low. After this, don't ever try to contact me again. If you do, I will tell Jah what you did and I won't be responsible for what he does to you."

"Okay. I guess I'll see you in a few."

Jazmin didn't bother saying goodbye. She ended the call and put her car in reverse.

After driving a few seconds in silence, Tanya asked quietly, "Are you gonna tell me what's going on."

Jazmin glanced down at her phone at her receiving texts. She slowed down to respond while saying to Tanya, "I'm gonna tell you in just a second."

On the ride over to Lamar's house, Jazmin filled Tanya in on what happened. She made Tanya promise not to tell Jah. After hearing what Lamar done, Tanya was livid and was ready to kill him herself. But after she saw who met Jazmin at the apartment complex, she knew there was no need to get her hands dirty.

Jazmin stood patiently outside Lamar's door and knocked. She wished she could erase the anger from her face but it was impossible. She couldn't offer any smiles when Kyomi answered the door. She wasn't expecting Kyomi to be there because Lamar said she wasn't there. But the show had to go on.

"Can I help you —"

Jazmin pushed her way into the apartment with her companions right behind her.

"Where is Lamar?" Jazmin asked flatly.

Kyomi looked at the others with Jazmin. She was nervous as she called out, "Lamar! You have guests!"

Lamar came from the back. When he stepped into the living room he hesitated but tried to smile although it was a nervous quiver of the lips.

"Hey," he greeted. "Abe, Landrus, Mr. Pavoni and Mr. Mancuso...what brings you all by here?"

Luciano looked at his big face Audemars Piguet watch impatiently. "Let's get this over with shall we. Jazmin, you have a nice day doll and we'll call you later."

She smirked at Lamar as she turned away and to walk out of the door. "Sure."

———

The following week Jah walked out of the Justice A.A. Burch Building a free man. All charges were dropped and he was happy beyond words. It was now time for him to move on with his life but in a more positive direction with more structure and purpose. Deep down, he was scared and unsure, but he was also anxious to be what he needed to be for Jazmin and Genesis.

He squeezed Jazmin's hand in his. She squeezed back and threw him an assuring smile.

She asked, "How do you feel?"

"Shit, I can't even describe how I feel right now," he told her. With thought, he said, "I feel like I got anotha chance though. Sheena would be tellin' my ass that this a sign for me to do shit right."

"You will. It's not going to happen overnight and it's a progress but we can do it together," she told him.

"Jah!" Rock called out. He hurried to join them. "Whatchu finna get into?"

Jah looked at Jazmin and shrugged, "I don't know."

"We need to celebrate this shit or somethin'," Rock said.

Cassie walked over to where they stood outside the building in its front courtyard. "I'm hungry. Yall hungry?"

"I am!" Jazmin piped. "Where everybody else at?"

"They're coming," Cassie said. She looked at Jah and grinned. "I know your butt happy."

He smiled, "Yeah."

Jazmin turned to Jah and broke out in a big knowing grin. "You owe me buddy! That hair!"

Jah shook his head emphatically. "Man, go the fuck on. I ain't cuttin my hair."

"We made a bet. So you're going back on it Jah?" Jazmin teased.

"You finna make that man cut his hair?" Rock asked.

"I told him if he get off he had to cut his hair since he just knew he was about to do some time," Jazmin explained. "Shouldn't he own up to his end?"

"Hey, it might be a good thing," Cassie said with a shrug. "Time for a change Jah."

"Fuck yall," Jah sneered. "I ain't cuttin' my fuckin' hair."

Jazmin narrowed her eyes at him playfully, "That's not fair. You owe me."

Cassie's phone rang. She answered it, "Whatchu want?"

Jazmin looked at Jah and asked, "What about the other thing?"

"We'll talk," was all he told her.

Jazmin lowered her voice and said seriously, "Well it's something I need to tell you."

"What?"

"I don't want you to be mad at me though," she said.

"Tell me."

"I'll tell you when we—"

Cassie interrupted them. "Oh my God! That was Tanya. She said Rayven just went into labor and they don't think the baby gonna make it!"

Although Rayven wasn't her favorite person, Jazmin's heart still ached for her. She called Desiree. The ladies agreed to meet at the hospital to be there for Rayven.

Trying to understand and not be so insensitive, Jah told Jazmin to go ahead and that they would talk later. She kissed him bye before going with Cassie.

The ladies waited patiently in the maternity ward's waiting room. Rayven's mother, aunt, and a close female cousin was there also. Knowing the friction between the ladies, Rayven's family remained to themselves.

"Nobody tryna talk to they asses no way," Tanya snarled.

"Hush," Desiree censured.

"Look at 'em. They over there acting just like Rayven's stank ass," Tanya hissed.

"Did her mama speak to you?" Jazmin asked Desiree.

"No," Desiree sighed.

"Who cares," Cassie said with a roll of the eyes.

"Is that Sean's son with them?" Jazmin asked in reference to the little boy sitting quietly with the aunt.

"It gotta be," Cassie said. "He look just like Sean. Can't even tell Erica's his mama."

When they saw Rayven's mother getting up, it caused them to see what was going on. It was Sean walking towards Rayven's mother and cousin. They exchanged words then the mother's shoulders dropped with devastation.

"Awww," Jazmin sighed heavily with sorrow. "She lost the baby."

Rayven's mother, aunt and cousin all headed to Rayven's room. Sean looked over and saw his former friends sitting there looking back at him.

"Hey ladies," he said quietly. "Didn't know yall were out here."

"Yeah, Ricky told me what was going on. Ed told him," Tanya said. "Thought we'd come out to give our unsolicited support."

Jazmin side eyed Tanya with suspicion. "Ricky huh?"

Tanya cut her eyes and said under her breath, "Shut up."

"So how is she?" Desiree asked.

"She's...she's a little crushed right now," he answered.

"How are you?" Jazmin asked.

He shrugged looking down at DeSean standing next to him. "I don't know."

"Probably happy," Cassie said under her breath.

"Do you think she'll wanna see us?" Desiree asked.

"I don't know," Sean said.

"What happened?" Tanya asked.

"I don't know," he echoed.

"Well what do you know Sean?" Cassie asked impatiently. "And don't say 'I don't know'."

Rayven's cousin, Allison came back into the waiting room. "Sean, your wife is asking for you."

Before Sean could respond, another man came rushing around the corner. "Allison! Where is she? Is she alright? Is the baby okay?"

Allison's mouth opened to say something as she looked from Sean to the other guy.

Desiree gasped. "Oh shit!"

"What is it?" Tanya wanted to know.

"Uhm," Allison started. "Michael, Rayven lost the baby but this is her husband Sean."

Michael looked at Sean and extended his hand. "Hi, I'm Michael, Rayven's boss."

Sean looked down at Michael's hand like it was diseased. "Why are you worried about me and my wife's baby?"

Allison tried to intervene. "Sean, Rayven wants you. Michael, why don't you come with me?"

Ignoring Allison, Michael said, "Actually Allison, I'd like to see Rayven. I know she needs me; *our* baby didn't make it."

The four ladies' mouths dropped open as they ping ponged between Sean and Michael.

"What do you mean our baby?" Sean asked angrily.

"Let me fill you in on something," Michael started but was interrupted by a right hook to the chin.

Sean was heated but he still felt the pain of his punch shoot through his body. Before anyone could put a stop to it, Sean and Michael were going at it. Security was called and came running.

Jazmin, Desiree, Tanya and Cassie sat there getting an eyeful of all the action. Once it was dispelled and the spectators all seemed to move on about their business, the ladies sat there quietly. They looked at each other, then burst into laughter.

"Let's get the hell up outta here!" Tanya laughed.

Desiree caught up with Allison. "Can you tell Rayven that we came by? And can you tell her Desiree said she knew she was a whore."

————

Later that night, Jazmin relayed the whole scenario out to Jah. She was so tickled by it all.

"I guess Sean had it coming," Jazmin said as she crawled into bed. "I mean, what did he think Rayven was doing while he was out doing him?"

"You mean while he was out doing yo ass," Jah corrected.

At a different time, Jazmin would have taken offense to Jah's statement but it didn't bother her. She joked, "Ay! I wasn't who he was with during all of that time. With so many women in rotation, I can only imagine how much time Rayven had to do her own dirt."

"So who won?" Jah asked.

"It was a tie I guess," she said. "They both were pretty whack."

Jah turned to his side to face her. "Don't tell me you feel sorry for that nigga?"

Jazmin gave it some thought. "You know what? I don't feel anything. It was funny though.

And come to find out, that's the same guy that was dating Abe's ex. He has this thing for other men's women. He and Sean are a lot alike."

"That's fucked up."

Jazmin reached out and pulled one of his dreads. "When are we going to the barbershop?"

Jah smiled, "Never."

"That's okay," she jested. "When you go to sleep I'm chopping them all off."

"And I'ma beatcho mufuckin ass," he said playfully.

"You won't be able to," she said. "You're going to be too busy crying."

"Too busy crying," he mocked. "Yeah like you bout to be soon as I put this dick in ya."

Jazmin rolled her eyes. He came at her before she could even think about getting away. They played around in each other's grip which eventually led to intimately touching and kissing. They were interrupted when Jazmin's phone started ringing.

She grabbed her phone and answered, "Hello?"

"Turn it on channel five!" Tanya said excitedly. "Hurry up!"

Jazmin told Jah to change the channel. There was a State Farm commercial on. Confused Jazmin asked, "Why you got me looking at a commercial I've seen a thousand time?"

"No, the news finna come back on."

"Who is that?" Jah asked.

"It's Tanya," she answered. The screen flashed back to the news.

Police have identified the two bodies that were found two days ago along the Cumberland River just past the Clarksville Pike bridge as Lamar Porter of Nashville and Kyomi Himura of Japan who was in town visiting. Though the bodies were discovered Tuesday, authorities believe the two were killed anywhere between Sunday night and early Monday morning. Police are asking the public to help in identifying a suspect in this heinous crime. It hasn't been confirmed if this incident has been connected to the city's recent reports of hate crimes against members of the LGBT community, but police have confirmed Kyomi Himura as being a transgender male. If anyone....

Jazmin's mouth dropped open in shock. A sinister giggle accidentally escaped her lips as she whispered, "It wasn't a hate crime though...well not in that sense."

Tanya said, "Bitch, yall going to hell!"

"You've got your nerves!" Jazmin retorted.

Jah asked, "Ain't that yo boy?"

"Uhm Tanya, let me call you back," Jazmin said and quickly ended the call.

Jah was in shock. "Damn, what the fuck happened to they ass? That nigga was just eatin' super salads at O'Charley's."

Jazmin shrugged, "I don't know. I think I'll reach out to his mama and give my condolences."

Jah wasn't quite sure how to take Jazmin's lack of concern. He watched her get comfortable in bed with indifference. "But that's yo boy. You don't seem upset like yo ass was when Tanya called bout Rayven."

"Do you really want me to be upset over Lamar?"

"No, fuck that nigga. But this ain't like you. Yo ass usually be on some 'let's save the unicorns and niggas with noodle dicks' bullshit. Lemme find out I'm rubbin' off on yo soft ass," he teased her.

Jazmin delivered her best Jah impersonation with an exaggerated attitude. "How 'bout you shut the fuck up and put that dick up in me like you said you was, nigga."

Jah started laughing. "Don't ever do that shit again!"

Jazmin joined in his laughter. As her giggles subsided she looked at him completely aware of how lustful she was feeling. She caught her bottom lip in between her teeth and stared at him with intense lust.

"Don't be lookin' at me like that," Jah said as he eased back.

Before he could escape she threw the covers back and pounced him. Pretending to be helpless, he let her manhandle him with kisses.

Jazmin pulled away. Still straddling him, she sat up. "I love you Jabari."

"You don't love me; you just love my doggy style," he said quoting a line from a popular rapper.

She giggled, "I love that too."

Seriously Jah said, "You know I've been thinkin' bout that marriage shit. I talked to yo daddy again and—"

Jazmin's eyes grew big with excitement. "You talked to Daddy again?"

"Yeah. I also talked to Abe about the shit. Damien tried to give me his two cents…didn't ask for it though—That nigga weak than a mothafucka! I don't wanna be like his ass. Desiree be running the fuck over his ass all the time."

"I'm not Desiree."

"I know…but that's the type of shit I think about. I don't want stuff to get crazy with us."

"It won't. But look," she said to assure him, "I don't want you doing anything that you're not totally sure about."

"But ain't it real to be a lil scared even though you know it's something you want?"

Jazmin's face scrunched up in thought. It relaxed but her eyebrow shot up in revelation. "Jah? Are you growing up on me? Lemme find out I'm rubbing off on your hard ass."

That made Jah laugh. This was something different between him and Jazmin. It was certainly something he had always wanted but to actually be living it was almost unreal for him. Or maybe it was the way the swell of his heart felt. It was different and scary but worth experiencing.

"Let's do it," he told her.

Jazmin moved off of him and went for her panties.

Jah chuckled shaking his head. "Not that…I mean, yeah that. Go 'head and take them shits off anyway. But I was talkin' bout gettin' married."

"Are you sure?"

"Yeah. Might as well. I ain't plannin' on goin' nowhere 'less yo ass get to trippin on a mufucka."

Jazmin shrieked with excitement. "When?"

He shrugged. "Whenever you want to."

A thought halted Jazmin's excitement. She asked, "Can we do it now?"

"You don't want no wedding?"

"I do want one but...," she let her voice trail off.

"But what?"

She shook her head and offered him a small smile, "Nothing."

He sat up and pecked her on the lips. "It's whatever you wanna do."

She nodded, acknowledging his comment.

"Ay, what were you gonna tell me earlier?"

Jazmin had to think about what he was asking. Once she remembered she looked at him timidly. Cautiously she began to tell him the secret she had been keeping from him. He didn't interrupt her as she explained. Once she was done they sat in silence.

Jazmin finally asked meekly, "Are you mad?"

Jah shook his head. "Yo ass shoulda told me this back then though."

She lowered her eyes with shame as she spoke quietly, "I was afraid because...because you were pulling away, didn't like the idea of marriage...and you just didn't seem like it was what you wanted."

"But it's you Juicy," he told her sincerely. "If it had been some other random stank booty bitch, I woulda been mad. But not when it comes to you. And I don't 'preciate yall keeping that from me. I shoulda handled that nigga."

"I just didn't want you in that position Jah."

He gave it some thought. He told her, "I understand."

"Well how do you feel about it?"

He smiled at her and stated, "I already knew."

.

Chapter 14

A week later, Jah awakened on July 31st anxious and excited. This was the day he was taking a vow to be somebody's husband. After they discussed Jazmin's secret, it was decided that they were going to take a trip downtown to the county clerk's office and go before the justice of peace to get hitched. It was something that would only be knowledgeable between the two of them. To everyone else, it would be announced that they had intentions to marry and Jazmin would start her wedding plans.

"Are you ready?" Jazmin asked that morning.

"Are you?" he returned.

She winked, "I've been ready."

Jah was really enjoying this new vibrant and confident Jazmin. Even the extra weight gain he noticed, but didn't dare speak of, didn't stop her. He liked it. It made her much sexier to him.

"So I'm taking Genni to my aunt's right?" Jah asked for clarification.

"Yeah, I already asked her," Jazmin said as she headed to the bathroom. "Jah, please don't be late either. You gotta meet me before two but two is our scheduled time."

"I'll be there," he mumbled.

"When is your appointment for your hair?" she asked.

"Aw shit," he hissed. "I needa get ready for that."

Jazmin stepped back into the room. She gave him a sneaky look.

He said, "What?"

"Cut it!" she laughed.

"Don't start that shit."

"I'ma leave you alone," she said going back into the bathroom. "I think I'm gonna cut mine today. I want something different."

Still too comfortable to get out of bed, Jah said, "You can cut that shit all off and you'd still be my Juicy."

"Aw! How sweet but you know you wouldn't want me baldheaded…But I am thinking of something layered like a bob. You think I'd look okay with that?"

"What I just tell yo ass?"

Jazmin started laughing. That's when he also heard Genesis crying from across the hall. Allowing Jazmin to continue getting ready for the day, Jah went and tended to Genesis. By the time

Jazmin came out of the room, Mittenz and Sox were ready to handle their outdoor business.

Jazmin and Jah kissed their goodbyes before she took off for her special day pampering. She made sure to remind him once again about the time. He promised her he would be there.

As soon as Jazmin left, Jah wasted no time getting himself and Genesis ready. He didn't want to upset Jazmin nor disappoint her in any way. He had to be on time. As a matter of fact he wanted to beat her there.

After dropping Genesis off with Georgia, Jah headed straight to the barbershop. A bet was a bet and he owed Jazmin. He thought he would surprise her and show up at the courthouse dreadless. He couldn't wait to see the expression on her face when she saw him.

Around noon, Georgia called him informing him that he didn't send not one diaper with Genesis. His mind was completely on Jazmin and getting to that courthouse. He had to laugh at himself for forgetting to pack diapers. Instead of going back home, he stopped at a store to grab a box. He had less than a full two hours to meet Jazmin.

Pulling up in Georgia's driveway, he received a text from Juicy: **My hair is done and Ling Ling is painting my toenails**

He text back: **make sure she get tht lft pinkie toe tho...dat mfcka dead**

Juicy: **FUCK U!**

He chuckled as he hopped out of his SUV. He glanced towards Nivea's house and the car parked behind her Cruze looked too familiar. He dismissed the thought and headed to the porch. He knocked on the door. Seconds later, Georgia opened the door holding a fussing Genesis.

"Boy! I thought you was Dewalis out here! You done cut'cho hair. What made you do that?" she asked while grinning the whole time and checking him out. "Genni, look at your daddy looking like your granddaddy for real now."

"Juicy won a fuckin' bet so I gave in and did this shit," he told her.

"You look good!" she beamed. "You look real good."

He blushed while rubbing his hand over his new tapered cut. "I ain't tryna look like that nigga De though."

"Well he is your daddy Jah."

"So. That nigga ugly."

Georgia shook her head. "Well you go on and have a good time with Jazmin. I gotta take care of this baby of yours before she cuss me out. You hear all this noise she making?"

"Aight Auntie," he said pivoting around. A car door slamming shut capture his attention. Then he heard her loud voice.

"Naw bitch! That ain't the shit you was saying while you was locked up and crying!" Tanya screamed as she stormed towards Nivea's porch.

"Tee, get this chicken head away from my house!" Nivea hollered.

"Man, both yall bitches messy," Tyrell said as he headed to Nivea's car. "Yall can argue by your damn selves."

"No! You can't use my car!" Nivea objected marching down the steps of her porch. "Go with her and yall get away from my house!"

"I don't want his ass!" Tanya stated loud and clear. "I just need him to be a father to Tyriq. He can be over here with you and yours and don't give a fuck about his own flesh and blood."

"But why come to my house? I ain't got nothing to do with that," Nivea pointed out.

Jah stood there and watched them go back and forward for a minute before he called out to

Tanya. "Man, get'cho ass away from that dumb ass broad's house. Fuck both them stupid mufuckas. And why the fuck ain't none of yall at somebody's goddamn job!"

Tyrell shot Jah a murderous glare. "How 'bout you stay yo ass over there!"

"Shut up Tyrell and just leave," Nivea said rolling her eyes.

Tanya slowly started heading back to her car. She said, "You know what? You right Jah. I don't even know why I wasted my damn time coming over here. I'll see you in court Ty."

"Fuck you fat bitch! Is the lil mothafucka even mine," Tyrell sneered.

Jah was still stuck on the part where Tyrell thought he could just talk to him any kind of way. Georgia had come back to the door and could see the darkness clouding Jah's face. She said, "Jah, don't go over there. Take yo ass and get in that truck and go to your woman."

That's what he should have done. That part of him that just couldn't back down, didn't want to back down. It was like he had the good of him on one shoulder telling him, *Don't go over there*, but then there was the bad of him encouraging him, *Go over there and beat his mothafuckin ass!* Then it all happened in a flash.

Georgia stepped out on the porch and called, "Jah! Don't do it."

When Tyrell saw Jah approaching, he said, "Nigga, ain't none of this going on over here got a damn thang to do with you. So walk yo happy ass on back—"

"Who the fuck you think you talkin' to!" Jah barked. His cool had left that quick as he rushed upon Tyrell.

Tanya hurried in between the two men. She pushed Jah as hard as she could, "Jah, he ain't worth it!"

"Then why you gotcho monkey ass over here!" Jah shouted at Tanya.

"You right. I shouldn't be here," Tanya said in a calming tone.

Jah glared at a smirking Tyrell. "What the fuck you lookin' at black ass ugly mothafucka!"

"Listen to your lil fat friend nigga," Tyrell sneered. He added, "You over here for her right? Or are you really over here cause of that hoe ass bitch over there." He pointed towards Nivea. He returned to his daunting tone. "Oh yeah, that bitch told me yall was fuckin'. She thought it was gon make me feel some type of way I guess. I really don't give a fuck. The bitch used up any—"

Nivea stepped to Tyrell full of bravery. "Then why won't you leave Tee! If I'm all these hoes and bitches you love calling me, then fucking leave!"

"I leave when I get good and goddamn ready."

"He ain't got nowhere else to go," Tanya interjected.

"Who asked yo ass to talk fat bitch?"

Tanya whipped her head in his direction, "Fuck yo stupid ass!"

Nivea hastily walked off heading to her porch. "I'll just call the police and they'll make you leave."

"Call the police if you want to!" Tyrell threatened. Nivea ignored him and walked right into her house. Tyrell turned his attention back to Tanya and Jah. "Both yall needs to get off my property."

"Jah!" Georgia called again.

"Go on over there to yo mammy nigga," taunted Tyrell. He gave Jah a menacing stare.

That was enough to unleash the beast. Tanya knew it too and there was nothing she could do to stop it. She was almost knocked to the ground as Jah attacked Tyrell.

"Goddammit!" Georgia cried with defeat as she watched the two men fight. Tyrell didn't go down easily. He actually hung in there longer than expected. But Jah managed to catch him with a left punch right cross to the ridge of Tyrell's chin with enormous force. A punch like that was too overwhelming that Tyrell had no choice but to shut down.

Tanya watched with fright and amazement as Tyrell's body dropped to the ground lifeless. But that wasn't enough for Jah. He began stomping him while slewing obscenities and threats for future encounters.

"Jah, that's enough!" Tanya cried for him to stop. She didn't want to walk upon him while he was in that zone for fear of being hit herself. Then she heard the quick "whoop whoop" of one marked police car. She looked toward the street and heard the veering sound of tires of two unmarked cars pulling up fiercely. Jah didn't hear them. He was still trying to bash Tyrell's skull in.

Then everything just seemed to slow down. Tanya continued to call out to Jah until an officer forced her out of the way. Nivea came out of her house and onto her porch. Thinking Tyrell was dead she started crying hysterically. Unable to get Jah's attention, two police officers drew their guns out demanding that he stop beating the unconscious man on the ground. A female officer rushed to Nivea's aide.

Georgia rushed over frantically, "Jah! Baby, get up! That's enough!"

"Ma'am!" an officer barked. A gun was turned to Georgia causing her to pause and throw her hands up.

"That's my nephew," she cried.

Jah bolted up, "Yall betta get them mufuckin guns out my auntie's face!"

"Jah! No!" Georgia warned him.

"Get on the ground now!" the officers ordered Jah with their guns still drawn.

There was no need in fighting it. Georgia pleaded through tears, "Jah just get on the ground. Don't...don't...Just do what they say."

Five minutes later, Jah was handcuffed and being handled roughly as they pushed him towards the marked car. He was arguing with the police although Tanya couldn't make out what he was saying. The siren of an ambulance had arrived on the scene to tend to Tyrell. Another officer was trying to question Tanya but she was trying to see what was going to happen to Jah.

"Tanya! Who's Tanya? Are you Tanya?" an officer asked her.

"Yeah," she mumbled.

He motioned for her to come over to the car before they forced Jah inside.

"Give my shit to my auntie," Jah told her.

Tanya took the things the officer handed off to her that came from Jah's pockets. The small cubed jewelry box threw her off. Jah looked at her finally with a hint of remorse, shame and gloom. As the officers shoved him in the patrol car Jah managed to say, "Give that to Juicy...and tell her I love her...and I'm sorry."

Then Genesis' cries tore through the air. Jah looked over to the side of him and realized Georgia was still standing on her porch holding his daughter.

There were no police, there was no ambulance, Tanya and Nivea were still going at it, and Tyrell was still standing. Jah had never crossed the yard. The good of him danced victoriously on his shoulder.

It was as if Genesis had to make her own plea to her father. Her cry snapped him out of it and it reminded him that if he allowed Tyrell and that whole situation before him to take him out of the peaceful place he had just gotten to, then everything that he and Jazmin were working towards would have been in vain. He was a work in progress but he knew the changes he needed to make in himself weren't going to happen overnight. However, this situation before him was a perfect opportunity to put his self-control to the test.

Jah scoffed with a slight laugh. He shook his head. He said to Georgia, "Them mufuckas dumb as hell."

"Yeah, but let them have that," Georgia reminded him.

He called out, "Tanya, getcho ass in the goddamn car and take yo ass home. Yo snotty nose son need a father figure, shit I'm here. Just make sure that lil mufucka got some Robitussin or some shit I can give his lil ass."

Tanya didn't want to but she had to smile while cutting her eyes at Jah for talking about her son.

Jah gave Tyrell a once over with a look of detest to let him know he wasn't about shit before he hopped in his truck. "Fuck this dumb shit; my Juicy waitin' on me."

Epilogue
Five months later...

Desiree's pregnancy progressed although it was considered high risk. She was put on bedrest very early. She and Damien were on good terms and was eagerly awaiting the birth of their daughter.

Although things didn't work out between her and her son's father, Tanya was still hopeful in finding the right man. Tyrell had proven to be a deadbeat. And even though Jah offered to be a father figure for Tyriq, it wasn't necessary. Ricky had been doing a good job of that. Their relationship wasn't comparative to Jazmin and Jah's but it was getting there. They were still friends and sexual intimacy hadn't even been explored. Tanya wanted to make sure it was what she wanted. Ricky respected that and it didn't deter him from seeing her consistently.

It took up until two months ago for Cassie to let her guard all the way down when it came to Rock. With his new job, money in his pocket, and a car Rock had become more and more desirable. His life had definitely improved and she could sense a surge in his confidence. He was still childish but she managed to look over it, especially when she sat back and witnessed him being a father to his two kids. One of the kids' mama she could deal with, the other one she couldn't stand. They had words but for the most part Rock tried to keep them away from each other.

Rayven and Sean were divorced. Initially Rayven was apologetic but realized things could never be the same between her and Sean. Besides Michael had given her an ultimatum. She chose Michael. Sean was outcast. He and DeSean lived with Michelle who had just given birth to Sean Jr. She was happy but he was miserable. To add to his misery, Sabrina recently told him she was pregnant.

Dewalis was still living comfortable in Jah's condo. He was diligently trying to compensate what he did wrong in Sheena's and Jah's childhood with doing everything right in Caiden's. As far as Gina...She crossed paths with another man just twenty years her junior with his own money. She left Dewalis. He met another lady closer to his age and began dating her. However, he kept messing up because whenever Gina came around...he couldn't resist.

Nivea stayed with Tyrell. She wasn't exactly happy. It shown in her face every time Georgia tried to speak to her from her house. Finding the situation hilarious and deserving, Georgia would wave and snicker every time she caught Nivea coming out of her house. Nivea would never speak back.

And Jazmin and Jah...

"Juicy!" Jah's eyes widen. He looked at her then back in between her legs. "His mufuckin head is right there!"

Jazmin cut her eyes at him angrily. She manage through a groan, "Shut up Jah!"

"Okay let's get ready to push again!" the nurse ordered. She looked at Jah, "Hold her leg."

"I can't," Jazmin panted shaking her head emphatically.

"Jazmin, you can do this sweetie," Phyllis said tenderly on the other side of her.

"Mrs. Bradford," Dr. Bradshaw said calmly. "We need for you to push."

"Yo ass better mufuckin push," Jah commanded. "My mufuckin son can't fuckin breathe stuck like that!"

Off to the side, Tanya and Cassie laughed. Paul shook his head, "That boy ain't got a bit of sense."

On the nurse's cue, Jazmin exerted downward pressure while squeezing Phyllis' and Jah's hands. It felt like her whole bottom was about to come out.

"Hold it!" Dr. Bradshaw ordered before quickly moving about in between her legs.

Breathing hard, Jazmin's eyes went to Jah as he quietly watched what Dr. Bradshaw was doing. A look of worry seemed to cross his face as he glanced towards the nurse. She wore an indifferent look because it was her job not to alarm the patient, but Jazmin had to know if something was wrong.

Just as she was about to open her mouth to ask, the nurse went back in drill sergeant mode. "Okay push as hard as you can! This is a big baby and we got to get these shoulders out."

Bearing down, Jazmin let out a roar to assist the force of pushing the baby out. And then a sense of relief waved over body. Dr. Bradshaw's hands moved fast and then the next thing she knew she had a baby on her chest. Phyllis, Tanya and Cassie cheered with joy.

The baby started crying like it was an afterthought. Tears came to her eyes as she affectionately adored her son.

Dr. Bradshaw handed Jah the surgical scissors. "Go ahead Dad."

After cutting the umbilical cord, the neonatal nurses whisked Baby Jah away while Dr. Bradshaw continued to tend to Jazmin. The ladies along with Paul moved to that side of the room to get a good look at the baby.

Everyone else seemed to fade as Jah focused on Jazmin. Their eyes locked onto one another. She tried to maintain a smile on her face, but the more she tried the more her face contorted in an ugly cry face. She couldn't help it so she tried to cover half of her face.

Jah moved closer to her. He looked at her lovingly. Her silky straight hair had been pulled up into a knot upon the crown of her head. Her hair had a healthy radiant glow to it along with the bright and fresh gleam of her face. The weight gain from the pregnancy had made her face rounder. She appeared rather cute.

Jah leaned down and kissed her atop her head. She turned her face up to him and tried to smile again but the ugly cry face returned.

"Stop that," he whispered soothingly.

"We got a son," she said cried.

"I know."

Paul walked back over to Jazmin's bed and looked at them with question. He rubbed his chin in bafflement. "Jazz and Jah...I couldn't help but notice that they were calling her 'Mrs. Bradford'. The last time I checked she was still a Foster. Is there something you two need to tell me?"

Jazmin and Jah shared a look, and neither one of them could suppress the smiles that spread across their faces. That was all the answer Paul needed.

As the day progressed, Jazmin received visitors sporadically. And just as he done when Genesis was born, Jah didn't go anywhere and he stood guard over their baby, who they named Jabari Maurice Bradford, Jr. He was indeed a big baby at nine pounds and eight ounces.

Looking at his little one had him in awe. He couldn't believe he had a son now. Ja-ja and Genesis were only ten months apart and he knew the two of them would be a handful. But in that moment he was happy that they both existed. That was two kids now that would depend on him. His offspring that would look up to him for life's answers.

Before Jazmin even confessed that she was still pregnant, Jah knew she was pregnant with Ja-ja. He wished he could say it was all just from knowing her body but she had left evidence of the pregnancy out in the open. He saw a sonogram of one of her earlier ultrasounds when the doctor was monitoring the baby's development.

Although Lamar had tried to terminate Jazmin's pregnancy, he was only successful at ending one. At the time Jazmin had been pregnant with fraternal twins, therefore separate gestational sacs were present. Only one detached and terminated. Jazmin's body reabsorbed the remains of the miscarried one and the other one continued to thrive.

"Look Genni," Jah said pointing to Ja-ja as he lay in the glass bassinet. "That's yo brother."

"Gen!" Genesis shrieked. She grinned showing her small teeth and pointed at Ja-ja. She returned her finger to her mouth. She looked at Jah then pointed her chubby wet finger at him. "Gen!"

Jah chuckled. When Genesis tried to talk she just said her name "Genni" in some variant way.

Phyllis reached for Genesis, "Let me take her so we can get out of here and let Jazmin get some rest."

Jah kissed Genesis before handing her over. Genesis, Phyllis and Paul bid Jazmin goodbye before leaving the two of them alone.

Jazmin motioned for Jah to move closer to her. "Come here big head."

Jah obliged and sat on her bed beside her. "Wassup? You still hungry?"

"Are you gonna get me some Taco Bell?" she asked.

"Whatever you want."

She smiled, reached up and rubbed her hand over his hair and then she outlined the trim of his beard with her finger. She pecked his lips with a quick kiss. "You so handsome and so nice to me."

In that moment, Jah became aware of the warmth and fuzziness in his soul as he always felt whenever he was in Jazmin's presence.

"Thank you."

Jazmin looked into his eyes and saw that the rims of his lids were wet. Frowning with concern, she asked, "For what? What's wrong?"

"Nothing's wrong; everything's right. Thank you for finally giving me that."

She felt the lump in her throat choking her up. She smiled through it and said, "No, thank you for showing me a true love. You know sometimes I think back to when we were kids and teenagers just shaking my head at myself. You've always been the love of my life. I just refused to see it. I should have treated you better back then. I'm sorry for overlooking you and trying to find acceptance elsewhere. You were right there always willing and ready to accept me as I was and as I am. And sometimes I wonder if I had taken the time out to return the attention you gave to me, could that have steered you in a different direction. I don't know. But I commend you for trying to be better. I respect you and admire you for being the father you have always been for Genni even when we didn't know you were really her father. I adore the Jah that you are inside. A lot of people don't get to see it like you have allowed me to. And now I can honestly say that my eyes are opened to the very thing I could never see. You absolutely love me."

Jah dismissed what she said playfully, "Yeah, yeah...whatever. So when me and yo' mouf gon hook up."

Jazmin started laughing. "You're a mess!"

"And you love my ass; mess and all."

"Sure do," she said before they locked in a kiss that went beyond an appetite for sex. It was more. It was passion. It was absolute love.

And though the odds say improbable
What do they know
For in romance
All true love needs is a chance
And maybe with a chance
You will find
You too like I
Overjoyed, over loved, over you…
~~ Overjoyed, Stevie Wonder

Acknowledgments

Shew! I did it. It almost didn't get done but it did. Won't He do it?

Where do I begin? This whole Crush journey has been amazing. It was a bit overwhelming at first but I embraced it. Back in June of this year, when I was writing the first installment, I had no idea that Jah was going to win so many people over. And to think, I was going to write him having some sense and being quiet at first. I'm glad I went with my gut and changed him!

Major shout out to all of the readers that made Crush such a huge success. Because of Crush, my other work was able to get some exposure and now I have some really great fans. I love you guys! Yall keep me up even when I'm down. The constant mentions of my name, tagging me, coming in my inbox…It all encouraged me and motivated me. I welcome all forms of reader stalking! I absolutely love it! The support, love and interaction has been awesome!

I LOVE TO READ AND CAN'T HELP IT! Bookclub…As always, hey complainers! (Especially Sheila Robinson, Alyce Amor, and Tarina Wright) Yall know yall ain't right over there. You know that, right? To my own group, Poison Ivy Readers Group (PIRG)…thank you all for rocking with me and showing me love. This particular journey has only begun! To all of the authors that have shown me love, thank you, thank you, thank you! Your inboxes have meant so much to me. My PIRG admins, Yolanda Morgan, Tureko

Straughter, Alisa Denay, and Mona Altidort. Thank you ladies SO MUCH! You really have no idea what having you all in my corner means to me. I'm so grateful for you all. You've been encouraging, motivating, inspirational...and I thank you! Love you ladies on some real shit! And the lovely Carmen Johnson...For those that frequent The Official Crush Fanpage, that don't be me posting all of that crazy stuff. It be her!!! Yeah, Carmen I threw you under the bus. LMBO! But thank you! You do a phenomenal job. I don't know what I would do without your help.

To my new signees to my newly formed company, Poison Ivy Publishing, thank you for wanting to be down with PIP! You ladies are awesome and have so much great talent to offer the readers out there. I can't wait for them to get their hands on what you got cooking Mona, Novia, Semekia and Shakela. Awesomeness!!!

Delores Miles and Kimberly Olds Artis, words cannot truly express how much I appreciate you two. You both became my friend at different times, but they were at the right times when I needed you. You help me to see past the clouds and focus on just the slightest ray of light. Even if we don't communicate for days, your words of encouragement are always long lasting. Love you ladies.

And my publisher... Tremayne Johnson. I don't care what nobody say 'bout'chu, you a cool mufucka! Whenever I doubt myself or have worries, you always reel me in. Sometimes you gotta slap some sense in me via inbox, but I eventually get it. Don't sweat the small stuff; focus on the bigger picture. I get it! As always, it's a pleasure working with you. With you in my corner, I now know there's no reason to be afraid.

Of course I still think you're awesome and you're wonderful at what you do. #ForeverKash To the rest of my King Publishing Group family...hey!

Shout outs to my mother Brenda Lockett, my cousin Geneva Mitchell, sister Ebony Woods, daughter India Bradford, daughter Harrah, son AJ, and son Dion for being encouraging and believing in me. Love you guys!

Made in the USA
Middletown, DE
04 March 2017